KISSING THE BEE

Also by KATHE KOJA

straydog
Buddha Boy
The Blue Mirror
Talk
Going Under

Kissing the Bee

kathe koja

Frances Foster Books
Farrar, Straus and Giroux
New York

Copyright © 2007 by Kathe Koja
All rights reserved
Distributed in Canada by Douglas & McIntyre Ltd.
Printed and bound in the United States of America
Designed by Nancy Goldenberg
First edition, 2007
1   3   5   7   9   10   8   6   4   2

www.fsgkidsbooks.com

Library of Congress Cataloging-in-Publication Data
Koja, Kathe.
    Kissing the bee / Kathe Koja.— 1st ed.
        p.   cm.
    Summary: The stress of finishing high school and preparing
for college is compounded for Dana as she comes to realize that
her best friend, Avra, is not the "queen bee" she has always
seemed to be, and that Avra's boyfriend Emil might actually
prefer a humbler "worker bee" like herself.
    ISBN-13: 978-0-374-39938-2
    ISBN-10: 0-374-39938-7
    [1. Interpersonal relations—Fiction.   2. High schools—
Fiction.   3. Schools—Fiction.   4. Bees—Fiction.]   I. Title.

PZ7.K8296 Kis 2007
[Fic]—dc22
                                        2006037378

My thanks to Frances Foster,
Rick Lieder, Janine O'Malley,
and Chris Schelling, for all
their help and guidance

... I
Have a self to recover, a queen.
—Sylvia Plath, "Stings"

I knew that change was coming, the way you know things you can't see, by feeling them; by instinct. The way the bees know everything they know.

Dana Parsons
Bio II 6th hour

The Society of Bees

Think of a bee colony, or hive, as a city, thousands of bees working and living together as a society. Most of them are female, nonreproductive, worker bees: these are the bees you're used to seeing, out flying and foraging among the flowers in your backyard. Then there are the drones, the males: far fewer of these, living their short but necessary lives. And in every hive—the one fact everyone knows about bees—there is only one queen.

Which in our little three-person hive was Avra.

• • •

"Is Avra coming over?" my mother asked, dumping corkscrew pasta into the boiling water. "Do you think I should make some extra?"

Avra had said she was coming; was she? Maybe. Probably. These days I couldn't always tell. "I don't know."

"Well," dumping in more pasta anyway, "if she doesn't, then I'll have it for lunch tomorrow."

That's my mother: the optimist, no matter what the facts may be. I'm not that way at all—I'm a realist. I respect the facts.

I know we're supposed to fight, that whole mother-daughter attachment/detachment thing, like Avra and her mom, but actually my mother and I get along pretty well. Maybe because we're so different. Maybe because it's been just the two of us for such a long time, since my father moved away, and then died. That was in third grade, long before I knew Avra, or met Emil, so far back it was another, separate life. Before and After, except I could barely remember Before. . . . Someday, this will be Before, too.

The pasta foamed and bubbled, then settled down to a steady boil. My mother started plucking leaves off the basil on the windowsill over the sink. The stained glass suncatchers, dream-catchers, sparkled and swung as her hands reached through them to the slim green of the plants. I read another page in the bee research book and made a note—*propolis, a sticky resin used as a fastener in the hive, like insect duct tape?*—past all the doodles and lists already scrawled in my notebook: *Emil get industrial scissors—sequins—cardboard at drugstore? MORE TAPE!!!* I should have been done making project notes by now, I should have had the whole thing almost finished, but. But I didn't. When my phone trilled I answered it on the first ring. It was Emil.

"Hey," he said. "It's me."

"Hey," I said. "I know. Did you get those scissors?"

"Yeah."

"Where are you?"

"Um, on your street, almost. Turning the corner. It's starting to rain. . . . Is Her Highness there yet?"

"Is she coming over here now?"

"That's what she told me."

As he said it, I almost thought I heard her car, that second-gear downshifting grind; there was something wrong with her transmission, her dad kept telling her to take it in to the dealer but she hadn't yet. *Before I go,* she said to him—I was there when she said it, standing half a step behind her in the TV room, looking past the French doors into the lemon light of the backyard, the beds and beds of her mother's roses, her mother wins prizes for her roses. *Before I go, I will.*

He thought she meant, what? Go to the prom? Go to college? Go to the drugstore to dig cardboard out of the dumpster? but *All right,* he said, and let it drop.

If her mom had been there it would have been a big long disquisition, all the things that could happen when you drove around with a faulty transmission, how much the car had cost, why Avra was essentially just a child and although this was not completely a bad thing, still since she was now a senior in high school, she might want to stick her head up into the real world once in a while and see what was actually what. . . . I liked Avra's dad. He was the one who taught me how to drive, even though my mother had paid for me to do it through school. But the school instructor had always confused me and made it hard for me to figure out what exactly she wanted me to do: *Left, OK now, keep your tires turned in—no IN—* as I'm sweating and yanking the steering wheel back and forth, thinking *In where?* I got the stupid certificate, I got my license, but I was too nervous to actually go out on a road and drive.

So one afternoon Avra's dad took me to the community college parking lot in his ocean-blue BMW, switched seats with me, and said *All right, Dana, put it in drive.* And I did. Around and around the parking lot, forward and reverse, parallel park, then up and down the access roads, until I felt safe enough to drive all the way home. He taught Avra the same way. Probably Shira, too.

When Avra said go, she meant GO. Out of the house, school, town, all of it, out and far away. The plan was she'd have everything she needed packed and ready in her car, and as soon as prom was over—she wasn't going to wait for commencement, she wasn't even going to the hotel after-party—then *zoom,* goodbye. Her parents wouldn't notice she was gone until the morning after, late morning, because they'd figure she was still at the hotel, but by that time she'd be far away. She had a couple of destinations in mind, maybe Portland, maybe New York, maybe even down South, she wasn't totally sure yet. *Savannah's supposed to be really pretty*, she'd say, her head back against the car seat, her eyes almost closed. *Or Hilton Head. That's an island, right? Think how cool it would be to live on an island.*

She'd been wanting to leave for a long time, since tenth grade, almost; no one knew about it but me. We'd talked about it a million times, in her room, my room, driving around, at school, everywhere, one big conversation that was always the same: *It's my life*, she'd say, drinking a smoothie, smoking a cigarette, staring up at the ceiling or the flowing green shadows of the trees. And every time she said it she'd frown, making a crease between her eyes that looked exactly like her mother's, although I never pointed that out. *My life. Why should I have to live up to anybody's expectations?*

She thought of her world, the world we both lived in, of school and grades and friends and parents, as a kind of game, a game she'd gotten sick of playing because she'd won and whoo-hoo and so what. Tall-blond-beautiful, check. Popular, check. Clothes and car, check. 3.76 GPA and enough (but not too many) extracurriculars, check. *Do you see what I mean?* she'd say, she'd demand. *None of that is*

MY life. *None of that is mine. . . . You know what I mean,* she'd say. *Dana, you're the only one.*

I did know. My life wasn't really like hers—I didn't have the two-parents-older-sister family, the big house and new car and all that—but enough of it was the same, so I understood. Even though I didn't see things the same way she did, I mean I didn't believe what she believed. I always knew that my life was my own.

And I also knew that there's no such thing as running away: she could go wherever she wanted, but her life would go right along with her, she would be just as close to everything as she was now, just as stuck, with just as many expectations; her own, too. So nothing would change. But I never tried to talk her out of it, no matter how many times she brought it up, and lately she brought it up all the time. I mostly stuck to the specifics.

So what are you going to do? I'd say to her. *For money.*

Well, I have my Visa. And eventually I can get a job, like at a 7-Eleven, or a thrift store or someplace. It would be kind of cool to work in a thrift store, don't you think? You could go through the stuff first, before it ever gets on the shelf. Or like in a vintage shop—

Your parents will go hysterical. You know that, right?

Let them, she'd say, and blow a long stream of smoke into the air. *They'll still have Shira. They'll always have their precious Shira.*

There was never any point in talking to her about

Shira. *Well, but what about college? and a degree, and everything? That stuff still matters, you still have to go—*

I can always go later, there's no law that says you have to go to college right out of high school. Sometimes it's even better to wait—like what Ms. Keener's always saying, right, "Don't go to college if you don't know what you're going there for." I haven't got a major or anything yet. And, poking me, *I don't have a big filthy scholarship like you do, Miss Einstein.*

You have a scholarship, you—

Not like yours.

That was true. I had a scholarship to Central—not a free ride, but a smooth ride—for science writing. No one seems to know what that is, so I hardly ever talk about it, but basically if you're good at science, which I am, and you can also write about it in a way that regular people can understand, which I can (that's called "communicating the findings and implications of current research"), then you get to stand in a fairly short line with money at the end of it.

My mother was happier about the scholarship than I was—I was just glad to find out that there was an actual name for what I could do—so happy that she told everyone about it a hundred times: Avra's parents, my aunt and uncle in Connecticut, all our neighbors; it was embarrassing. And anyway "It's not like I couldn't go to school without it," I said, because that was true, had been true for a long time, since the settlement from the accident, sitting there untouched in the bank but "That's not the point," my mother said. "This is something you earned, not something someone just handed to you."

"No one 'handed' the settlement to us. Someone paid for that. Dad paid for—"

"Oh, Dana. You know what I mean."

People were always telling me I knew what they meant, and it was almost always true. I was getting so incredibly tired of that.

Emil was the first person I'd ever met who seemed to know what *I* meant. All of it. The first and only person.

The power of the bee is a uniquely female power, held by the queen bee and the female workers who do the bees' hard work of survival: gather up the pollen, feed the larvae, protect the hive. In myth, the Queen Bee symbolizes the Goddess, the High Priestess, and the worker bees are her vestal virgins. Ancient statues of Artemis, the Greek goddess of the hunt, were adorned with the power symbol of the bee, as were other goddesses like Cybele, Demeter, and Rhea, the Greek Earth Mother, and the Mother Goddess in Minoan culture. It was once believed that a virgin girl could walk right through a swarm of bees and never get stung, recognized by them at once as being one of their sisters.

Shira was a year and seven months older than Avra but two years ahead of us in school, because she was born in

December but Avra was born in July, or some technicality like that. So she was a sophomore at Acosta College while we were finishing up at Addison. I forget what her major was, but this summer she would be interning for these urban-archaeologist people. It actually sounded pretty interesting—you go into a dilapidated city neighborhood and try to figure out how it got that way, why it crumbled, not to jump in and fix it, but to understand. Like you can't cure a disease just by knowing the symptoms, you have to know what's causing those symptoms first.

Anyway. Avra's parents talked about it all the time, how proud they were of Shira, how they were going to go visit her on-site over the summer, if she could spare the time to see them. I don't know if they ever asked Avra to go along with them or not. Not that it would have mattered. Not that she would have gone.

Shira was always doing things like that, interesting things that Avra would never think of doing in a million years. Like all through school, Shira had hair practically down to her waist, this frothy white-blond mane, but over the holidays she cut it all off, as a donation for Heavenly Hair, you know, the ones who make wigs for sick people. Her mom cried, and her dad said she looked as beautiful as Audrey Hepburn. Avra didn't say anything, just ratted and sprayed and lacquered her own hair until it looked like a tumbleweed, a huge sticky ash-blond basketball with a face in the middle. And she wore it that way for a week, until it was impossible to brush into shape anymore, and even smelled a little. It took Emil half a day to shampoo all the crap out and comb it straight and clean. I sat on the toilet lid and read out loud to them from *The Best of Johnny's Bathroom Humor* as they sat in the tub in their wet T-shirts and shorts, rinsing and scrubbing; it was the only book I could find. *What did the fisherman say to the traffic cop? What's the best way to get down off an elephant? Why did the doctor put iodine in his coffee?*

It wasn't that Shira was mean to Avra, or looked down on her; no more than any big sister looks down on any little sister, I guess. It was just that she was always *there*, older, blonder—not taller, Avra was the family Amazon—and *bigger*, always bigger. It made Avra love Emil immediately when he didn't know who Shira Travis was, or swoon when he finally met her. I mean, he thought Shira was pretty, because she *was* pretty; she was beautiful. But it was Avra he wanted.

I wanted Emil. I wanted him from the very beginning, before Avra even saw him. No one knew this, even though Avra would occasionally make these odd little jokes, when we were all together: driving somewhere, the radio on and the windows down; or sitting on the patio, under the acacias; or drinking gunpowder tea in our favorite booth at the Green Bowl: *If anything ever happens to me,* she'd say, piling my hand and Emil's together on the lacquered green table, his long fingers, the scarred silver-spoon ring she gave him, *you two have to carry on in my name.*

Carry what on? I would say, sliding my hand back, my skin electric where it had touched his, a living tingle.

It's the least we could do, Emil would say. And roll his gray eyes, and smile.

His smile is so sweet. Always with his lips closed—there's this little gap between his front teeth, extremely cute but he is very self-conscious about it—long narrow lips the exact shade of Dark Peach lip balm; his hair is the color of champagne. He is just as tall as Avra but only just. My head barely comes up to his chin. . . . Once he slept with his head on my shoulder, in the backseat of Avra's car. We had gotten bored at this stupid keg party—neither one of us is much of a drinker—so we went out to the car to wait for Avra, waiting and yawning and talking and then not-talking, until Emil finally just gave up and fell asleep. His hair—it was longer then—mashed up tickling against my skin, his arm was warm and still and heavy on mine. I took little breaths, tiny little breaths, to breathe in his smell, to not break the spell and wake him up. The streetlight shone sideways through the back window, that faint underwater green, and I pretended we were on the ocean somewhere, on a sea journey, a nonstop honeymoon cruise. I leaned my head sideways, craned it sideways, so my hair would brush his. Finally I fell asleep, too.

When I woke up I was all hunched up against the door, with a terrible neck-ache, and Emil and Avra were in the front seat together. I pretended I was still sleeping, even though they weren't paying any attention to me, even though it felt like I was falling into the deepest hole in the world, a hole opening up inside my chest, deeper and deeper every time they made a noise, soft wet noises, every time Emil moaned or Avra whispered *You*. You, you.

She said it again now, in the pasta-scented kitchen: "You," to Emil sitting there beside me, his T-shirt damp from the rain, the notebook open between us on the table, the bee book closed. She kissed him on top of his head, a preoccupied, throwaway kind of kiss; she kissed me the same way, actually. Then she hugged my mother, an extravagant, too-long, clenchy hug: "Janis, hey. I brought you some flowers," half a dozen perfect white roses, some in bloom, some just budding, jammed into a Mountain Pure bottle. My mother oohed and aahed, then set the bottle on the counter.

"I'll put these in a vase later. Avra, you're so thoughtful. . . . And you're just in time for dinner. Emil, you're eating, yes?" as she started filling a plate for him.

My mother is actually a fairly wonderful cook. She pretty much makes the same things over and over but they're always good—pasta and pesto, a cheese-and-walnut ravioli, a Thai kind of stir-fry—and every time a tiny bit different. *Variations on a theme*, she'd say.

Sometimes we had wine with dinner, but never when Avra or Emil were there. Today there was Pellegrino, and naan, which is a kind of Indian bread, and as we ate, Avra talked: about her half day at Camp New Horizons with the eighth graders, teaching them not to panic about going to high school next year; how Kellie Ballister and Amy Dane had a huge fight in swim class, and Kellie threw Amy's phone in the pool; about how the minute Avra walked in the house, her mother started up again, another letter had come from Acosta admissions, she could get in right now as a legacy but there was no place on earth she would rather go less: "I'd go back to Addison for another year," Avra said, talking with her mouth full. "I'd go back to *middle* school. Or get a job at SavMor. . . . Are we going to Sav-Mor?" she asked Emil and me, in the way that wasn't asking, she knew we were, she knew she wanted to.

"Where are you headed after high school, Emil?" my mother asked. "To Central, like Dana?" Emil just ducked his head a little, and smiled.

Once Avra and Emil fell in love, there was no question that he was going to go with her, run away, I mean. I don't know if Avra ever actually asked him, or if she just took it for granted that he wanted to go wherever she went. He had a partial scholarship to Central, not as good as mine but still pretty OK. But whenever Avra talked about leaving, he would nod.

I wasn't going; Avra hadn't asked me to. Even before Emil, she never asked.

The creation of a new queen is extremely important to the hive—without the queen, there will be no honey, no colony, nothing at all—so anywhere from two to twelve queen cells might be constructed. As the new queens are about to emerge, half the colony may leave with the old queen, massing and waiting on a nearby tree or bush while the scouts find a safe location. Then the swarm follows her to their new home.

At the old hive, as the first of the proto-queens, or "virgins," comes out of her cell, she makes a sharp high-pitched noise that the others, still in their cells, hear and answer with little cries of their own. She moves through the hive, looking for her sisters, tracking them by that noise, and kills every one of them, unless one of them kills her first. Sometimes all the virgins die from their battle in-

juries. But the battle is necessary. There can be only one queen in the hive.

When Emil first came to our school last fall, no one really knew what to think of him. He was hot-looking, but not in a normal, magazine-guy kind of way, not in the way people were considered hot-looking at Addison. He played no sports, he played no instruments, he signed up for no groups. He was nice to people but not particularly friendly, or needy, or cool. He was just *there*, sitting in the quad at lunch, eating chips, watching us watch him. The whole first week I kept staring at him and thinking, Today I'm going to say something to that guy, I'm going to go over there and say, *Hi, I'm Dana.* Then I thought, how stupid would that be? It would be better to just say *What's your name?* or *What school are you from?* or *Do you like it here at Addison?* And while I was observing him, and considering all these things, Avra came back from her family's reunion vacation and walked right up to Emil and said, *You. Who are you?* And that was that.

It's not like I never had any boyfriends of my own. Actually I was a lot more into the whole hooking-up thing the first few years at Addison: who was with who, who did what at whose house, who missed her period, who was going to break up at lunch or the dance or first hour Monday morning. All the gossip, all the buzz.

But by junior year, I had kind of, I don't know, burned out on it all. It was like being on a ride at the carnival, lots of thrills and chills, but you always ended up right back where you started. You'd think, *Oh, this is it, this time I'm really going to fall in love,* and then it all would just . . . shrink and dwindle, until you didn't care anymore, and then you'd realize you'd never really cared about the guy in the first place, it had all been a waste of time. Another waste. So I stopped dating altogether. Then I stopped going to the parties and the concerts and the keggers. Then I stopped going out at all.

My mother noticed me getting less and less social. First she thought it was because I was bored with school or my life or something, then she thought I was depressed and ought to go talk to somebody even though I kept telling her nothing was wrong, and I wasn't going to "talk" to anyone, I was fine. So then she started saying things like *Just wait—the world will open up for you in college, Dana, you'll see.* Then she'd give me all these examples of how that had happened for her: how she did forensics and was really good at it, and went on summer trips to Paris with all kinds of wonderful people like her roommate Solange, who's still her friend to this day, and met my dad on a bridge at midnight, and so on and so forth. And I'd sit there and look at the sun-catchers in the window, the dream-catchers, deep blue, warm canary yellow and think, Well that's you, Mom, that's not me.

Which was why Avra made a difference. Avra was different from a best friend, she was basically what I did. I know how that might sound—like I'm a sheep, a sidekick, glad to lap up her sloppy seconds. But it wasn't like that at all. It was true that she was kind of—well, very—high maintenance, and true that we mostly did what she wanted to do, but. *But Dana,* she would say as we sat on the patio listening to music, or smoked out the window in the guest room, or Shira's room when Shira wasn't home, or did one of our road trips—once we drove all night to Elder Dunes, ran out to splash in the lake, then turned right around and drove like crazy to get back in time for school—*Dana,* she'd say, *you are my mind. Without you I'm just a brainstem.* She meant it, too. Not that I was smarter than she was, but that the way I saw the world, my philosophy, was like her road map. She would ask me constantly what I thought about things, did I like this person or that person, did I think she should take the Films of the '60s class, did I think we ought to register to vote or protest by not registering or forget the whole thing or what. Before she made a move, she asked me first.

In fact I was the one who decided what she and Emil should be for the senior prom. This year's theme was "Bal Masque," as in masquerade, and everyone was going crazy trying to get their outfits together; it's not that easy to find elaborate costumes when it's not Halloween. Kellie Ballister's mother was having her dress made, this whole Marie Antoinette outfit, a satin dress with lace and a train, and a powdered wig: *Just like George Washington,* Amy Dane said. Amy Dane and Will Lopez were going as Cinderella and Prince Charming. Kyra Worth and Jason Columello were going as the King and Queen of Hearts, like the playing cards. Avra and Emil were going as a butterfly, one butterfly, one wing for each. Made out of cardboard, white gauze, iridescent pink sequins, and duct tape.

Which is why they, we, needed all that cardboard from SavMor, and the industrial scissors; the duct tape was Avra's idea. You'd be surprised how many colors duct tape comes in: silver, of course, and white and blue and yellow, but you can also get it in hot pink, and mint green and other pastels, and a metallic brownish-copper almost the exact same color as my hair. We went to every craft store we could find. Avra's whole car smelled like tape.

Now "Just wait till you see our costume," she said to my mother, scraping her fork against the plate. Rain speckled the steamy windows, water inside and out. "Janis, you will just *flip out*, you will just *die*. Everyone will die when they see how amazing we look."

"It'll make for a lonely prom," Emil said, and I laughed. My mother smiled.

Avra frowned. "That doesn't even make sense," she said.

Emil had sketched a bunch of costume ideas in my notebook, strange beautiful things like aliens and wild creatures, costumes no one could ever make, or at least we couldn't. One afternoon, a few weeks before, he and I sat in the dining room at Avra's house and I watched him draw, as Avra and her mother screamed at each other on the patio. They were arguing about choosing a college, but it could have been about anything; that's the way things were between them these days. Actually ever since Shira left, they'd been fighting, while Avra's dad escaped into the TV room. Avra kept saying, *You act like the world ended when she left. But I'm here. I'm still here.*

Emil was slouched sideways on one of the armless dining room chairs, hair tucked behind his ears, wearing his Red Cat Orchestra T-shirt. He sketched casually, like it was nothing, like anyone could draw the way he could. It was fun just to watch him. *That's so beautiful,* I said, as the drawing filled the paper. I meant him drawing, too, but he didn't know that; I'd known he wouldn't know that.

It's supposed to be our butterflies, he said. *The way they grow in stages, meta—, what do you call it. Metamorphosis, that's butterflies, right? what they do? What do bees do?*

Bees?

We didn't speak for a minute, Avra yelling loud through the glass doors—*just like Shira, you never listen to anything I say, you never fucking—*

Avra, lower your voice! Avra—

We looked at each other again. *Well, you're always reading about them,* Emil said. *I figured you would know.*

It's for Bio. My final project.

Mr. Davis, the Bio II teacher, doesn't believe in tests and quizzes, or even really in homework: he believes in Projects. You take a million notes all semester—you'd better—and then you make a Project about whatever it was you were supposed to be learning. But you can't just come up with a list of facts, you have to be creative, you have to *build on what you KNOW*, you have to *exTRAPolate*. Mr. Davis talks like that, in CAPital LETters. *I don't want regurgiTAtion*, he always says, tapping his pen against his desktop. *Show me you LEARNED something.* That semester's unit was on cooperative societies. I was kind of tired of human beings by that point, so I decided to do bees.

He likes facts, I said to Emil. The sun through the patio doors made his hair glow, a pale halo around his face. *CreAtive facts. Like, did you know there can be over 80,000 bees in one hive?*

Emil raised his eyebrows. *Whoa. That's a lot of honey, honey.*

He erased the antenna on one of the butterfly-people, and drew it again, an elegant feathery arc. The butterfly-people were tall and gorgeous, holding hands; mirror images. Perfect for each other. He frowned, and erased the antenna again. *So do bees do metamorphosis, too?*

No. Drone, worker, queen. Work, mate, fly, make honey, die when winter comes, all but the ones at the center, the ones clustered with the queen in the deep heart of the hive. Nobody goes to prom, or college, nobody drives off into the sunset, nobody's world opens up. *Bees pretty much are whatever they are when they're born.*

Then I'd rather be a butterfly, Emil said, shading one creature's face, delicate pencil lines. *I'd rather change.*

Don't change, I thought, please don't ever change. But I didn't say it. Then Avra slammed back in, shivering the glass door, crying, and we had to go.

*A*s shown in the photo and diagram (Fig. 7), the egg that the worker bee comes from is identical to that of the queen's. But the queen larvae are raised in different, peanut-shaped cells, and are fed more royal jelly (sometimes called "bee milk") than the worker larvae, so the queen grows much faster, and completes the growth cycle in approximately sixteen days. For a worker bee, the cycle is longer, but on the twenty-first day, the young worker bee finally bites through the capping on her cell and emerges into the comb, to begin her lifetime's work.

Everything necessary for the correct functioning of the hive—constructing the combs, defending the colony, collecting and processing the honey, raising the young—is the task of the worker bee.

The colony's success depends on her as much as it does on the queen.

Does any worker bee actually believe this?

I deleted that last part, though.

Now in the car, the last of the rain and Avra was crying again, but happy tears, sniffling along to "All the Way to You"; it was the big song that year; it was our senior class song, too, the predictable choice. Our class colors were the same as the school colors, silver and a kind of dark teal; how lazy is that? Apparently there wasn't a lot of imagination happening on our Senior Committee. Avra was on it, but she never went to any of the meetings; she was voted onto the Prom Committee, too, but she never went to those meetings either. She said, *Who cares what stupid hotel they pick? I won't be there anyway.*

Our class motto was "Together, We'll Reach the Stars." Dorie Huber, who sits behind me in AP English, said the motto was so idiotic that she was considering boycotting commencement altogether. Dorie Huber could have been valedictorian, or at least salutatorian, but she deliberately got an A-minus on a physics test to drop her GPA one-thousandth of a point or whatever, so she wouldn't have to write a speech for morons. *You gotta be careful,* she said, picking at her white nail polish, little flakes and chips like snow around her, or plastic dandruff. *You get too shallow, you evaporate.*

I laughed, to be polite, but to be honest I couldn't imagine why she or anyone would care enough to get that incensed about any of it. It was only commencement, it was only Addison. It was only people in mortarboards and fake-satin gowns, just costumes like the costumes we were going to make tonight, pulling into the puddled SavMor parking lot, behind the building where the dumpsters were, the cardboard flat-folded and tied for recycling. Emil wrestled a big damp bundle of it into the trunk as Avra dabbed away her mascara, blue mascara, it left faint blue circles under her eyes.

"I *love* that song," she said, and lit up one of her herbal cigarettes; the scent was like burning flowers, not a bad smell but I got sick of it after a while. I put the window down. Now I could smell the dumpsters. I put the window back up. Emil slammed the trunk and hopped back in the front seat; he had a smear of something all down his Red Cat Orchestra shirt, wet and oily-brown.

"Goop," Avra said, pointing at it with her cigarette hand.

Emil looked down, saw the stain, made a face, pulled off

his shirt and threw it out the window. Faint goldish gleam of hair on his chest, just a little, up by his sternum, is that what it's called? where the neck and chest meet? His skin was lighter there than on his arms, a coffee-with-three-creams color. I could feel my heart beating. I wanted to touch him, put my hand on his chest and feel those little hairs, see if I could feel his heart. I had to look away then, stare out the window at the other cars, the parking lot, the drenched green light of the trees.

"I bought you that shirt," Avra said, frowning.

Actually she'd bought two, one for him and one for herself, but she took hers off and lost it somewhere, maybe in that disgusting ladies' room in the arena. It was a great concert. We sipped White Oak vodka out of a Mountain Pure bottle in the parking lot, and Emil and I danced to every song, until our hair was plastered to our foreheads and necks, and his new T-shirt was soaked. Avra drank so much she fell down in the ladies' room and lost her shoe somewhere in the slime, then threw up in the car all the way home.

Emil took pictures of her buying the shirt, yanking it on over her spangled tank top, half-inside and half-out, just wriggling arms visible, like a creature with no head. It seemed like Emil spent half the concert taking pictures. . . . The day after, Avra and I sat waiting for him to come out of Siamese Sisters with pad thai and lemon rice, because only lemon rice could cure her hangovers. She'd picked up his camera from the seat and *Let's look at Emil's pictures,* she said.

We started clicking through them: The club from outside, the long rowdy crowded line to get in. The T-shirt picture of no-head Avra. A picture of me, singing, sweaty. A picture of me, leaning against a wall. A picture of me, fingers over my eyes like in *Pulp Fiction,* the dance-contest scene. A picture of me, laughing. Neither of us said anything. She had that grooved line between her eyes again, faintly, and then when Emil got back into the car she said *Hey,* and the line got deeper. *You took like a million pictures, but they're all of Dana. Where am I?*

Well, Emil said, setting the bags carefully on the floor. He didn't look at either of us; I remember that. *You were sick, right, you were puking all over everything. Do you want pictures of yourself puking?* And then he took his camera back.

The next day at school, going into the media center, Avra stopped me in the doorway and said, *Would you ever . . . you know . . . hook up with Emil? I mean do you ever think of him that way?*

I looked at her. She had her hair pulled back in a ponytail, so you could see all of her face: pink forehead, blackberry lipstick, hazel eyes wide. She looked like a little kid somehow, like she had in sixth grade when she got Bs on her report card instead of all As, even though she'd tried as hard as she could. She looked—perplexed.

Why are you asking me that? I said.

Well why shouldn't I ask? Don't you think he's filthy hot?

Of course he is. So what.

So nothing, she said, the line alive between her eyes. *Forget it.*

That night she and Emil went out alone, not with me.

My mother asked me once why the three of us went out on dates together: that's what she called it, dates. *Isn't that kind of awkward?* She was at the counter slicing tomatoes at the time, with her back to me, deliberately, I think; I know. That's how she is, careful of your feelings. I was at the table picking cashews out of the little oval nut-dish, blue checkerboard dish, cracked pieces of cashew in the trail mix; I didn't answer. I thought of the three of us together, three parts of one thing, three components; is that what it was like? No. It wasn't like that at all.

I'm not criticizing you or anything, Dana, I'm just asking if—

I know. I just, I don't know how to answer you. I mean, it's not awkward. To us.

The knife made little sounds against the cutting board, *tap-tap-tap, knock-knock-knock,* something tiny asking to come in, or get out. *Well, I just wondered,* she said.

My mother never makes a big deal about anything, except possibly my scholarship. And when my dad died. She feels that life is so strange—she's told me this—life is so strange there's no sense in being surprised by anything. Anything can happen any time, she says. She even has it as a refrigerator magnet, black curlicue letters on fluorescent pink: ANYTHING CAN HAPPEN, in a circle, circling around inside itself.

Not all bees sting. The family Meliponidae is an order of stingless bees, who have developed other kinds of defenses to protect their hives against intruders. But when a bee does sting a human being, the bee loses its life. The stinger is barbed, and human skin is thick enough that the bee can't withdraw it once it has been inserted, so the bee struggles until it rips itself free, leaving the stinger and parts of its body behind. This is always fatal to the bee. The person who was stung merely has a sore spot for a day or two, unless that person is allergic to bee venom. Then the sting will be fatal both ways.

My father died because a man had some kind of argument with his boss, got incredibly drunk in the middle of the afternoon, and drove his Jeep Arroyo into the back end of my father's Honda at seventy-four miles an hour; the police said he never even tried to brake, they didn't know if he was suicidal or what. He didn't die, though. He got pretty messed up, but he didn't die. My father died. He never even made it to the emergency room.

My mother asked me if I wanted to go to the funeral with her, but I said no; I stayed at my grandmother's instead, staring at the TV while I colored my way through an entire coloring book she bought me, *Animals of the Alphabet*, I remember that. B for Bear. T for Tiger. Q for Quail of course, what would any of those books do without quail? Z for Zoo. I colored hard; the pages were soft and dented from the wax of the crayons, new crayons; I remember that, too. When my mother came to pick me up, my grandmother met her on the front walk and hugged her, and asked how the funeral had been.

Closed casket, my mother said.

Are you all right? my grandmother said.

I've been better, my mother said. Her fancy black blouse was all wrinkled. Her eyes were red. *How's Dana?*

I had come up behind them on the walk; I put my arms around her from behind and squeezed. *I've been better,* I said, and they laughed a little, kind of startled, and then my mother cried. At that point I hadn't actually seen my father for, I don't know, a while. But I still wanted to have him in the world. I was sorry the guy who hit him hadn't died. I didn't tell anyone this, but I was. I wanted it to be fatal both ways.

The insurance company sued for us, or sued for itself and we somehow got the money, I'm not too clear on the details; to be honest, I've never really cared enough to ask. All I know is that there was a settlement, and my mother put it in trust for me, for college. And now, since I wasn't going to need it all for college, I could get the rest when I was twenty-one, or twenty-five, or something. I didn't care enough to ask about that, either. The money was just there, like the roof on the house. And it didn't really make up for anything.

Once, back in ninth grade, not long after we started being friends, Avra asked me where my father was. *Like how come you don't go to his house on weekends or anything?* We were watching TV in my bedroom, me on the bed, Avra on the floor; *Borderlanders* was the big show that year, we both had giant crushes on Sean Swann. When I told her about the accident, she kicked my closet door so hard it left a mark we couldn't wash off; my mother had to paint over it. I loved her for that. I still do.

I wasn't going to the prom. When people asked—people at school, or my mother—I said I didn't really want to go, and it was true. When we first started talking about making the costumes, we joked about the three of us going together as triplets, the Three Little Whatevers, but that wasn't such a funny idea after all and so we dropped it.

It was like that one time when we double-dated, Avra and Emil and me, and Jason Columello, who was on the basketball team and sat across from me in AP English and wrote papers on Chaucer that I had to peer-edit. We had decided for some reason—actually, it might have been Avra's idea—that we needed somebody for me to date, and Avra said Jason had had a crush on me since forever and I should just ask him for some Friday night, just casually. I did, and right away he said yes.

So we all piled into Avra's car, them in the front seat, me in the back next to Jason Columello, who was wearing this weird extra-spicy aftershave or cologne, it smelled like something you'd use for a marinade. We went to the movies, some silly martial-arts comedy that Jason wanted to see, then over to Avra's to sit on the patio and drink beer. I could tell that Emil didn't like Jason: he kept making little remarks like *Hey, you first, big guy* or *I bet Jason can do those kinds of martial-arts moves no sweat, right Jason?* I didn't like him all that much either, to tell the truth. He laughed all the time at everything whether it was funny or not, he drank most of the beer, and he had very big wet pink gums. I realize that mentioning his appearance is shallow, not a reason to dislike someone, but still. We dropped him off first, and Emil kept fake-laughing, *haw haw haw* and baring his teeth, his gums, and I laughed, too, and Avra got mad and said we were both being immature and unfair: *Jason was trying as hard as he could,* she said.

And Emil said, *Yeah well you shouldn't have to "try." Not with Dana.*

• • •

That was the first time I really wanted to kiss him. The first time I thought about it, imagined how it would be: my hands on either side of his face, that smiling mouth under mine. How he would taste. What he would say. What we would do.

I know how that sounds. He was Avra's boyfriend; Avra was my friend. *He's not for you*, I told myself, and I meant it. But he was still Emil. And I still wanted him.

> *Honey has served many symbolic purposes. As ambrosia, it was fed to the goddesses and gods on Olympus, to keep them healthy and forever young. In Celtic rituals, honey was sacred to the goddess Brighid, and used in the "bridal bed" rituals to represent fertility. In those ceremonies, a male chieftain and a female virgin of the tribe had sex on "Brighid's Bed" to insure abundant blessings on their fields and work. So honey could be thought of as an aphrodisiac, too.*

Sometimes Avra calls him "Email" or "E-Male," or "Lime" which is "Emil" backwards. He hates nicknames. He loves wasabi rice crackers and chocolate (not together). He hates having to be at school at 7:20 in the morning (well, we all hate that). He loves going to the midnight movies at the dollar show inside the crappy mall in Elleston, where all the stores are like cheap mirror versions of stores you're used to shopping at. He loves the little plush tiger Avra brought him from Montreal, a white tiger hand puppet, he keeps it on the bookcase by his bed. He loves sitting on Avra's patio at night and watching the moon through the acacia trees. He loves Avra.

I love gunpowder tea and chocolate (not together). I love writing that explains why things happen. I hate writing about Chaucer. I hate when Jason Columello and his friends look at me in the hallways and say stuff that I can't hear. I love watching Emil's hair blow and tangle in the breeze from the car window. I love watching the moon through the acacia trees. I love Emil.

Avra, wake up . . . *Avra.* Hey."

"What?" The pillow crushed over half her face, one eye peering, cranky like a little kid is cranky. When Emil and I got there, at eight-thirty like we'd all agreed, her mom rolled her eyes and said "Her Highness is still sleeping— just go on up." So now we sat on either side of Avra's bed, ankle-deep in T-shirts and ashtrays and crumpled magazines and empty water bottles, each of us tugging on an arm like she was a rag doll, trying to wake her up: "Hey, Sleeping Beauty, come on. Time's a-wasting, we gotta go."

"No. What." She glared up from under the pillow, sky-blue pillowcase, her face all crinkled and lined from the sheets, her hair tangled and sweaty. "Go where."

"The apiary," I said.

"The *what*?"

"The apiary," Emil said. "Where all the apes live. Hnh-hnh-hnh," grunting like a gorilla, off the bed and shambling around the room, shoulders hunched, arms dangling; I laughed. Avra dragged the pillow back over her face. He gorilla'd a little more, crunched something underfoot, a plastic-cracking sound, made a face: *Oops*. Sat back down.

"It's the bee place," I said to the pillow. "For my project, remember? You said you'd help me take the pictures, you said—"

"No," she said, then said it again, louder, "*no*. I'm tired. Go without me."

"Come on, Avra," I said, "we'll wait for you. You can just hop in the shower and—"

"You can just *go*," she said, past cranky to bitchy and "OK," Emil said, and stood up. Right behind him, hung on the wall, was a picture of the two of them that I'd taken at Harsens Point, out on the ferry dock. She'd enlarged it so it was almost life-size; seeing it now was like seeing him in a mirror, a mirror of the present and the past and "Come on, Dana," he said, leading me down the stairs, past her mom who said "No luck?" and "Oh well" and as we climbed back into the car "She doesn't do much for you," he said, "does she?"

I shrugged. I wasn't mad; I wasn't even surprised. "You know Avra."

"Yeah," he said, "I do." As we pulled out of the driveway, he adjusted his sunglasses and "You guys have been friends a long time," he said. "Why?"

"What?"

"I mean, she's not usually a very good friend to you. Is she."

It wasn't a question, but I made it one. "Yeah, she is. She can be when she wants to." Why didn't he already know this about her? "She's your girlfriend. Isn't she?"

"That's different. . . . You two are such opposites." I didn't say anything, he didn't say anything, I turned toward the highway and "Onward," he said in a different voice. "To the gorillas. Gorillas in the mist. Where is this bee place, anyway?"

"I've got directions. Want to read the map?"

"You assume I can read. That's good. I like that kind of misplaced confidence."

So I drove, and he navigated—"Next exit, look for the turnoff, OK now go left"—from expressway to asphalt to gravel, careful with my mother's car, she let me keep it for the whole day *because it's for schoolwork* but it didn't feel like work, it felt like a holiday, a skip day, the two of us off together alone. He opened bottles of water, made jokes about the signs we passed; the wind blew his hair, the sun turned it gold. I thought of Avra with the pillow over her head and I was glad, so glad, so guilty and so glad.

"Are there any butterfly farms?" Emil asked, as we rolled up to the gate, TREEVILLE FARMS in carved-looking letters on a smooth wooden board, like at a sleepaway camp.

"I don't think so," I said. "They keep bees for the honey. What would anyone keep butterflies for?"

He thought about it for a minute. Then "The beauty," he said. "Just for the beauty."

• • •

Inside at the apiary, the owner or manager, the main guy, whatever—his name was Mitch—invited us to walk around and see everything, take pictures of whatever we wanted; he seemed pleased that I was researching a project about bees. "They're marvelous creatures," he said. "Absolutely marvelous. I've been doing this for sixteen years, and I learn something new every day." He was an older guy, my mom's age probably, with a neatly shaped brown beard and a really deep tan, like maple syrup.

He started telling us the basics of his business—how there were all kinds of commercial apiaries in the U.S., how much honey people ate in a year, how much his own bees produced—until he saw that all we really cared about was seeing the actual bees. So he gave us both beekeeper's helmets, white safari-kind of hats draped to the shoulders with mesh veils, warm and dim, and made jokes about not having coveralls in our sizes—"The beekeeper's body armor. They're 100 percent sting-resistant. Until they're not, ha-ha"—and about the smoker, which calms and distracts the bees—"I use hardwood chips, or sometimes pine. Maybe I should try something stronger, ha-ha." And then he pulled on work gloves, and very carefully opened one of the hives.

They were like stacked-up filing cabinets, rows of neat white drawers, but with life and bustle and struggle inside, the bees' universe of growth and work; and honey. Honey from the actual comb tastes amazing, not like anything you've ever had from a restaurant or a store. That honey is just the shadow of real comb-honey.

"This is *great*," Emil said. There was a fine line of sweat on his upper lip; his lower lip was glossed with honey. Salt and sweet. I looked down at my notes: *Bees are any of 20,000 species of insects belonging to the super-family Apoidea and the order Hymenoptera.* Pollination, propolis, Pliny the Elder. Bees as servants of the Earth Mother. Early beekeeping practices. "They didn't have drawers like this in the olden days," I said. "They used to weave skeps out of willow. And wicker. And daub them with clay."

"What's daub?" Emil asked.

"Well!" Mitch the beekeeper said. "You really have done your homework, haven't you. Take a look at this."

He led us to a storage shed and showed us some antique skeps, which are like munchkin houses in a cartoon, hobbit-houses, roundish and squat and "There's an entire museum of this stuff," he said, "in Scotland, I think. A whole museum dedicated to bees."

"It's in Edinburgh," I said. "They have a Web site."

Emil laughed. "Dana knows everything."

And all the while, as we ate the honey and I asked questions and the bees rose around us and settled, rose and settled, Emil took pictures; tons of pictures. Of the honeycomb and the hives, the flowers and flowering shrubs— Mitch had planted certain kinds for the nectar, so the bees wouldn't have to go far to forage: lavender, clover, fennel, dandelions, purple and blue and yellow, because that's what the bees see best. Pictures of the TREEVILLE FARMS sign, the outbuildings, the old skeps lined up on the sunny bench and "Now," Emil said, squatting down in front of me, "we need some pictures of you."

"No," I said. I could feel my face get pink. "What for?"

"At least one, Dana, come on."

"I don't have anything to do with the project—"

"Yes you do, you're writing it."

"Well it's not about me, it's—"

"To prove you were actually here, then."

"And that you didn't just download it all from some Web site, ha-ha," Mitch said.

So Emil took my picture, then a picture of me with Mitch, in the shade of a honeysuckle trellis that must have been twelve feet tall. And Mitch took a picture of Emil and me in the same place, then gave us a couple of jars of honey to take home, little fat golden jars with "Treeville" in script above a smiling bee in a tree.

Driving home took longer, partially because we got slightly lost—Emil had east and west confused for a while, so we went about half an hour out of our way, but it didn't matter, really, we weren't in any hurry to get back. We just drank our lukewarm water, and drove, and Emil asked me questions about bees, to quiz me, but he didn't know anything about them so he had to make it all up: "Do bees ever fly backwards? Can they be taught to climb little ropes and things, like in the circus? and ring tiny little bells, birdcage bells, wouldn't that be kind of cool? No? . . . OK. Do they mate for life?"

"The males do. Technically. But they don't really live very long."

"Poor guys."

"Very poor. They can't make wax, they can't make pollen, they don't have stingers so they can't defend the hive. All they do basically is mate."

"Well, that isn't all bad. . . . How many kinds of bees are there?"

"A lot." I took his sunglasses and put them on, the narrow black sunglasses he calls his obscurators. "There are like 20,000 species. Halictidae, Andrenidae, Bombidae. The bumblebee, the plasterer bee, the burrower bee—"

"I'm glad we didn't go see *them*."

"The honeybee—which is the only domesticated insect besides the—"

"Termite, like in that one commercial, right? 'Terrible Tim Termite / He only comes out at night—'"

"No, the silkworm."

"That's what we should have been for prom. Worms." He didn't say anything for a mile or so. I couldn't tell what he was thinking. Then "What's the difference between drones and worker bees? Aren't they the same thing? Whoops, sorry," as the water bottle tipped sideways between us on the seats, trickled slow and cool and "No," I said, standing the bottle back up. "Drones are males. Worker bees are female. They live to tend the hive and the queen."

"And they never get to mate, or be queens, or anything? Some life," Emil said. "I thought my parents had it bad, but that's ridiculous."

He talked a little about his parents then, about how they were like kindly but distant aliens, always busy with their work. They'd met at some university lab, and instantly fell in love because they were the only ones who could understand each other's arcane science jargon. They'd lived in China for a while, doing research, then moved to Minnesota, then Michigan, then here. "Romantic, huh," he said. "Work work work, it's all they ever think about, or talk about. I'm surprised they had time to have me."

I pictured them, his serious scientist parents, wearing lab coats, working diligently for the betterment of humankind, or whatever it was they were doing. "My parents met in Europe," I said. "On a bridge over some river. My mom said they were both slightly high at the time."

Emil laughed. "Now, that's romantic."

"Like a perfume ad," I said.

He didn't say anything for a minute, then "Avra told me your dad died," he said. "A long time ago, right?"

"Right. They were already divorced, I never really saw him anymore. —Am I going left or right here?"

"Sorry, sorry—I think left. Yeah. Left." I made the turn, he capped the water bottle. Then "Do you miss him?" he said. "Your dad, I mean?"

"No," I said, surprising myself, then "I miss missing him," I said. "I did when he was alive. Now he's too far away for that."

"You don't talk about it."

"I don't talk about a lot of things."

He nodded. We didn't say anything for another mile or so: just the sound of the wind, the purr and chatter of the radio. Then "I wish Avra was like that," he said. "She keeps talking about things way past where it can help anything. Or change it, or—I don't know." He rubbed his hands over his face, squinched his eyes open and shut. "I just get so *tired* of talking. . . . How do bees talk? They buzz to each other, or what?"

"They dance."

"Seriously?" He opened his eyes wide. "They dance?"

"Mm-hmm. It's their primary language. They tell each other how far they are from a nectar source, or from their hive, by two kinds of dancing. One's in a circle, that tells where something is generally, and the other is like, like wagging its tail, and that tells exactly where something is. Somebody even made a robot bee that can communicate with real bees by—Sorry. That's probably a lot more than you wanted to know."

"No," he said, "that's cool. Talking by dancing. Just filthy cool."

We didn't say much the rest of the way home. The sun moving through the sky, Emil silent next to me, not the silence that means you're deliberately not talking, but the silence that means you don't need to. The whole drive felt like honey, warm and gold and slow. I was so happy. I was just so happy.

• • •

It was almost eight by the time I dropped him off, there in the circular driveway, behind the gleaming little black car and "Thanks," I said.

"For what?"

"For going with me."

"It was fun." Out the door, giving me a little wave, then he turned around and came back, leaned in the window and "You know how bees could be perfect?" he said. He smelled like sun, and clean sweat; he smelled like Emil. "If they just had bigger wings. Like butterflies. Butterflies fly around and pollinate and get nectar and everything like bees do, right? But they just look so much cooler. . . . Put that in the project, OK?"

I smiled at his smile. "I will. If it fits."

I watched him walk up to his house, watched while he stood at the door, waiting? what was he waiting for? And he waved. And I waved, and started driving away. And he watched me go. . . . Was that what he was waiting for?

Did you put it in?" Emil asked me, as Avra drove us to school the next morning. "About the bigger wings?"

Avra looked at him, then at me in the rearview mirror. She had her hair in this complicated braid, wound around her head like a sleeping snake; she was in a snaky kind of mood. "What are you talking about? Our costume? If the wings are any bigger, we won't be able to fit in the stupid *car*, we—"

"Not that," Emil said. "Dana's bee project. Her big Bio project? . . . Hello, she's only been working on it for like two months. Don't you ever pay attention to anything that isn't you?"

She gave him a weird startled look, then glanced at me again. "What's the big deal? So I don't know about your homework, so what?"

"It's all right," I said.

"I don't know about yours, either," she said to Emil.

"Does that make me an evil person or something?" And she kissed him, a fast fierce little kiss. "Who cares about any of that stuff anyway? Pretty soon all that's over for us."

I knew what she meant, not *us* all three but *us* them, not *over* because school was ending but *over* because they were leaving. *Pretty soon.* Less than a month now. And all of a sudden I felt like I couldn't be there anymore, I wanted to, to jump right out of the car, jump and run and get far far away. But I didn't. We parked in the Student K lot like always, and we all walked into school together: Emil on one side, me on the other, Avra in the center. Like always.

The bee has two pairs of wings. The larger wing on each side is ridged with hooks that attach to the smaller, rear wing, converting four wings to two for flight. The wings unhook to become four smaller wings again when the bee lands. This is especially useful in the confined spaces of the hive. The bee's wings developed evolutionarily to enable it to perform its duties with the most efficiency and the least energy loss. Larger wings, like a butterfly's, while certainly more beautiful to look at, would be completely useless for a bee.

Avra called me on Sunday, early, early for her anyway, a little bit after eleven and "Just you and me, girl," she said. "Let's go."

For a minute I thought—I don't know what I thought. Then "Go where?" I said.

"I don't know, just *go*," so we did, just she and me and no Emil, she and me and a half bottle of wine under the seat, some kind of white wine she started swigging as soon as we pulled out of my driveway and "God, Avra," I said, "don't do that, we'll get pulled over. And it's way too early anyway—"

"Or too late," she said, and laughed, but she put it away, corked it and shoved it back under the seat. When we got to the stop sign at my corner, she reached over and hugged me around the shoulders. She smelled like wine and herbal cigarettes, like Chanson perfume; she was wearing Emil's Cardinal Rules T-shirt, wrinkled and too big. "You seem so, I don't know. . . . You seem sad, Dana. Are you sad?"

"No," I said.

"Don't be sad. It's Sunday, we have the whole day to burn. Let's—I know, let's drive out to the dunes again, want to drive to the dunes?" but first we had to stop for gas and then get cigarettes and then she had to swing by Siamese Sisters, she had to get a carryout of lemon rice because "I'm *starving*," she said, shoveling away with her spork.

"Or hungover," I said, but not like a question.

She looked at me over her sunglasses. "Don't be a bitch."

It was a beautiful day, like the apiary day, but. But it wasn't. For one thing, Avra drove way too fast, speeding up to red lights, then jamming on the brakes; then she played the radio too loud, singing along to all the songs; then she told me—for the third time—how Shira wouldn't switch rooms with her even though "She doesn't even *live* there anymore, for god's sake, that's how selfish she is. And my *mother*, my stupid mother won't even—"

"What do you care? You won't be there much longer anyway, right?"

"That's not the point. You *know* that's not the point. . . . What's wrong with you today? You act like you don't even want to be here." She nudged me with her elbow. She was smiling, a little sideways smile, very testing and—what's the word—tentative, like a little kid who's trying to see if you're angry or not. "If you don't want to go to the dunes, we don't have to, we—"

"The dunes are fine," because they were, of course they were but in the end we never got there, barely halfway, already four by the time we got to Rosedale, where we stopped at a Java Joint for coffee because she had to have a cappuccino, she had to tell me all about what her mother thought about making a costume for prom and why her stupid mother was wrong as usual and why her stupid mother didn't understand *why* she was wrong—

—and all the while I listened, I stirred my mocha crème, silver spoon like Emil's ring, the fake-sweet smell of the crème like the opposite of honey, the true honey from the comb. Like being with Emil was a true thing. . . . While he and I were together we talked about ourselves, but about other things too, like the bees, but with Avra you can only talk about Avra. It's really the only subject she has.

She's not a very good friend to you. Is she.

I just kept stirring, looking down at the tabletop, the smooth caramel-colored plastic, no seams, no end and "Dana, are you sad?" she said again but I wasn't sad, it was worse, much worse; I was bored. Totally and completely bored, by her, by her problems, by the way she just went on and on. And I felt so guilty about being bored that it made me instantly mad: at her, at myself, at both of us. It wasn't like before—once upon a time a drive to the dunes would have been the highlight of our week, once upon a time we were the center of our world no matter what, no matter who Avra was sleeping with, no matter who I was breaking up with, no matter what else we were doing. Was that over now? Because of Emil? No. Not because of him. But was he a symptom? a catalyst? or a cataclysm? Ask his scientific parents, I thought, ask yourself, you're the famous science writer, why don't you write about *that*? Write about centripetal force pulling you forward, centrifugal force pushing you away—

"*Hey,*" Avra's fingers snapping in my face, too close to my eyes, "Dana, hel-*lo*," I *hate* when she does that, I've told her a thousand times not to but she does it anyway so "Stop it," I said, dropping the spoon so it made a noise, faint metallic *ching*. "I heard you, OK? I always hear you."

She stared at me for a second, eyes wide, really wide, then "OK," injured. "You hear me. Now hear this: Let's just fucking *go home*, all right?"

We didn't talk on the way back, she had the music too loud and I had nothing to say. By the time we left the expressway she had pulled out the wine bottle again, drinking the last of it right in my driveway, on purpose, just chugging it down and tossing the bottle in the backseat. And saying "Bye-bye," in this hideously bitchy way, and roaring off into the twilight.

And that was that, except "Dana," my mother said. She was right there by the driveway gate, gardening gloves and clippers, she had been there all the time. "I hope I didn't just see what I thought I saw. And if I did, I hope it never happens again. *Ever.* You understand me?"

I didn't say anything. I knew she was thinking of my dad.

"Because that is not safe. It's a safety issue, it's—"

"I know," I said. "Don't worry."

"I'm serious, Dana."

I felt heat in my face, in my head, I felt like saying *Why are you yelling at me? I didn't do it, I didn't drink and drive like that guy that killed Dad, I don't even like drinking. Avra's the one. Why aren't you yelling at Avra?* But instead I said "I know," again, and slipped past her and inside.

I was so tired, as if I had been running all day, so tired I felt achy even after a warm shower. I was just going to bed even though it was early, not even midnight, but my phone rang, stopped, rang again, rang again. I knew without even looking who it was.

Before she said a word I could tell she was crying; hearing that made me feel even tireder, like I had thought I was done with a job and here was more to do, like standing at the top of a mountain and seeing another, bigger one right behind it but "Hello," I said, as if I hadn't heard it, as if I didn't know it was her on the phone although who else would ever call me crying?

"Hello," she said, through little gulps and sniffles, was she drunk? and "I couldn't sleep," she said. "I had to talk to you, I couldn't sleep."

"You know," I said, "you really pissed off my mother, she saw you with that stupid bottle. I told you not to do that."

Now she really started crying, mumbling, "Tell her I'm sorry, I *am* sorry, I didn't mean to, I just—Dana, you're not mad, are you? You can't be mad at me, you have to be my friend."

"I am your friend, Avra, you know that."

"Always. You have to be my friend *always*."

I wondered if she was home, out on the patio, in bed. Or in the car somewhere. I wondered if Emil was with her. No. "I'm your friend," I said again, my voice higher than normal, slower, and soft, like I was talking to a child. I felt like crying, too. Why? "Stop crying, OK? Just, just go to sleep."

"OK," she said. I could hear her blow her nose, a long wet sound. "You're not mad anymore, are you?"

"I'm not mad."

"Tell your mom, OK? That I'm sorry?"

"OK." And we hung up.

I didn't tell my mom anything; I went to bed. But I couldn't sleep, just lay on my back in the darkness looking at the glow-in-the-dark stars on my ceiling; I know they're really meant for little kids but I still like them. Pale green gleam, swirled and speckled, my own private constellations, *see your future in the stars.* When I did fall asleep, finally, I dreamed of them, glow-in-the-dark stars like streetlights, lining the sides of a road that I drove with someone beside me, was it Avra? or Emil? or someone else? I couldn't tell. It was too dark to see, even with all the stars.

One important way that bees maintain their colonies is by using pheromones. The worker bees secrete pheromones from a gland on their abdomens (Fig. 9, Nasanov gland). When the queen mates, she attracts drones by a different kind of pheromone, secreted from her mandibular gland. That same gland produces "queen substance," a secretion that worker bees lick from the queen's body and exchange one to another when they pass food. This queen substance inhibits the worker bees' ovaries, making them sterile. So one could say that their maintenance of the queen is their downfall— if the worker bees had any ambitions to be queen, which of course they do not, they would be a lot more careful about what they ate.

• • •

The costume ideas got less and less elaborate as we discovered how hard it was going to be to actually make any of them. None of us were the engineering type anyway, and once we started planning it out as real clothes that real people would wear, well. Plus it's not what you'd call a comfortable material: duct tape doesn't breathe, so you sweat, and it's a lot heavier than you'd think. Like being encased in plastic. At least that's what the dos and don'ts we downloaded said. *DO remember to leave access to zippers, so you can get some emergency air! DON'T forget, the tape can cause allergic reactions in some people.*

"Why are we doing this whole tape thing again?" I asked Avra.

"Because I fucking want to," she said.

Since we'd driven, or not-driven, to the dunes, she was like this more and more, harder and harder to deal with. Like every day closer to leaving made her less calm, more ready to argue and cry. Or both. Just like every day made me more silent, more—aware. The way you stop and hold yourself still, when you hear a noise you can't name: *What was that?* To put all of yourself into figuring out what will happen next. Even though ANYTHING CAN HAPPEN. But ANYTHING means only one thing, not all of them. Not EVERYTHING. For something to happen something else has to not.

For the dresses we went to the Sunshine Shoppe, the charity thrift store where all the Drama Club kids shop. It smelled like a cross between someone's garage and a plastic bag from the attic. We passed the housewares, the Tots' Department, the sports equipment, all the way back to the ladies' formal wear section that was sad and funny all at once. You'd see the clothes hanging there and think, Someone actually wore that hideous thing, someone had high hopes to look pretty, to have a good time, to be the belle of the ball. But now "It's the tar pit for old bridesmaids' gowns," Emil said, flicking through the racks as Avra tried on pair after pair of scuffed-up pumps. "Eventually they just melt back into the chemicals they're made from. Petroleum, and mercury—"

"And arsenic," I said. "Look at this one." Hideous grass-green spaghetti straps, sky-blue gown, with long wavy green midriff stripes to match the straps. "Only someone who truly hated you would ask you to wear this in public."

"Oh yeah. *The Revenge of the Color-blind Bride*." He swept a dress off its hanger, an actual bride's dress, and held it against him: yellowed skirt, fake glue-white pearls clustered thick down the sleeves. "Tell the truth, Dana dahling, is it me?"

"Oh it is. You look filthy gorgeous, dahling."

"Oh thank you, dahling. Kiss-kiss," leaning down to air-kiss me. I did it back with my eyes closed, kiss-kiss. I could smell his skin. His lips just brushed my cheek; I felt it all the way down my back, like an echo.

"Quit it," Avra said, frowning up from the shoe rack. "Be serious, you guys, we have to find something today."

We ended up choosing two dresses, one in case we screwed up too much with the first, and a tuxedo jacket for Emil; we still hadn't figured out how the wings were going to be anchored, though one of the dresses had a choker-kind of neckline with a big strap up the back and I thought we could maybe glue-gun the wing to that. Or sew it, though I wasn't much of a sewer, and Avra was even worse. Emil said he'd never actually sewn anything but was willing to try. "To tell the truth," he said, "I'm a lot better with nails."

We bought the dresses, we were heading for the door, when Avra spotted a gigantic black suitcase with all kinds of zippers and straps; it was sort of falling apart, its wheels were crooked but "Hey," she said, "this is perfect, we can use this when we go." She had a ton of suitcases already, her parents did, but that wasn't the point and I knew it and so did Emil.

So we stood by the door with the bags, waiting for her to go through the line again and "Are you ready?" I asked him. "To go, I mean?" We hadn't ever talked about it, them leaving, but somehow it just popped out.

He shrugged. He wasn't looking at me, or at Avra, he was looking at the figurines lined up on the display case, chipped glass Holy Marys with doves, rearing horses and bowing ballet dancers, a laughing red Buddha. "Yeah. I guess. My parents are truly not going to like it, but—You know, I don't even know where we're supposed to be headed? I mean I have no clue."

"Neither does she."

"I know."

"It's not about going to Savannah, or wherever. She just wants to run away."

"I know." He looked at Avra, still in the line; she wiggled her fingers at him. Kiss-kiss. I stared out the plateglass windows at the parking lot, the birds landing on the arc lights, the crushed-up fast-food bags. When she rolled the suitcase out to the car, Emil unzipped the main compartment and tried to fold himself small enough to climb in, then looked up at me, head bent sideways. "It's really more your size, Dana." He kept looking at me. For once I had no idea what he meant.

"Let's *go*," Avra said, and slammed the driver's side door.

Now we had the dresses and the jacket and the cardboard, a glue gun Emil dug up somewhere, all those rolls of tape, and some beer. Avra was the only one drinking, really, drinking and smoking, Red Cat Orchestra blasting away. We couldn't work in her room, there was literally no floor space that wasn't piled a foot deep with clothes or papers or whatever, so we spread everything out in Shira's old bedroom, on the shiny pine floors. She still slept there when she came home from college, so everything was mostly how she left it, emptied out and clean, just a few of her things still around: her Attic Giants poster, some half-burned aromatherapy candles on the dresser, mango and lavender and English rose and "Welcome to the shrine," Avra said. "Please feel free to light a candle to St. Shira of

Acosta, and pray to be as perfect as she is. Although no one ever can."

Her mom and dad were gone for the evening, to an Addison function, something to do with commencement. They were the very involved type of parents, volunteering for the school board and committees and PTSA and all that. My mother read the newsletters, and made sure to go to teacher conferences, but otherwise she wasn't much of a joiner. Emil's parents never went to anything because "All they do," he said, "is work."

"Worker bees," I said, flattening out the cardboard.

He nodded, solemn up-and-down, then suddenly smiled. "Which would make me a bee, too, right? Bee-boy. Son of a bee—"

Avra lit yet another cigarette. "You're not a bee, dummy, you're a butterfly. Half of a butterfly."

I didn't say anything.

I met Emil's mom once. I was driving Avra's car that day, I don't remember why, picking Emil up to go somewhere Avra already was. His mother was in their circular driveway, climbing out of her little black Mercedes with an armful of papers. She had very short hair, almost as light as his, and she was tall like him, with thin arms and bony wrists; she looked like a greyhound, nervous and intelligent and fast. As I pulled up behind her, she waved at me, an awkward waist-high wave, because of the papers, and smiled.

Oh hi, hello. How are you?

Fine, I said.

She paused; I waited. It lasted awhile. *How's school? It's OK.*

She made a funny little gesture, nodding toward the house. *Well. I'm sure Emil will be out in just a minute.* She blinked at me in the sun. Her eyes were like his, too, that same clear deep-set gray. Suddenly she smiled. *You know,* she said, *he thinks the world of you.*

For a second I just stared, then: She thinks I'm Avra, I thought. I felt my cheeks get red, but I didn't want to explain, I didn't even know how to start so I just smiled back and said *Thanks.* Two seconds later Emil came out and they kissed, little pecks on the cheek, which I thought was sweet.

Bye, he said to her. *I might be late, we're going out after the movie.*

Bye, she said to us both. *Have fun.*

As we drove away I said, *She's nice.*

Emil smiled a little, put the window halfway down. *Yeah. She's all right.*

Um . . . I think she thought I was Avra.

Emil pushed back the seat, and slipped on his sunglasses, his obscurators; then he looked at me. *She knows exactly who you are,* he said.

" 'Oh don't you know / Our lives are so / Very complicated . . .' All right, now how does this look?"

Avra was zipped into the choker-neckline dress, which

actually looked very good on, much better than it had on the hanger. She and I had striped the skirt with duct tape, carefully overlapping bands of pink and green and silver, although silver's not really a color you associate with butterflies, but then again this wasn't a science project. We'd used so much tape we were already running out of pink for Emil's jacket sleeves.

He was across the room, on his knees, his long body folded in half like a bent coat hanger. He was carefully cutting out the wings, using the big steel industrial scissors we, he, had borrowed from the art studio at school. The design he'd sketched, in careful black marker, was very complex. Complicated. One wing was half cut out, and creased already, a long sideways crease the wrong way. Slivers and chunks of cardboard were everywhere, on the floor, on him.

Avra kept on singing, tugging at the tape around the choker: " 'So come and walk with me / Down the long midnight road / Because I can't see the way when I'm walking alone, I can't seeeeee'. . . . This is *sticking* to me," she said, and grinned; a little bit drunk, more than a little; happy.

Emil said, "Shit."

"I'm going to wear those, you know, peacock feathers. For earrings, right? like we saw at that street fair? Because they look like butterfly wings, the patterns on them, the— eyes. I'll just have them dangle and brush against my shoulders. And for the corsage, Emil can get me a—"

"Shit."

"What?" Avra half turning, half annoyed. "What's the matter with you?"

"These stupid wings," he said. He had his back to us now. "They're so fucking big, it's almost impossible to— Would you turn that *down* a minute? I can't get this stupid—*Shit!*"

"What are you so cranky about?" Avra crossed the room to him, the dress rustling as she moved, graceful glide against the floor. It was just tape stuck to ugly polyester, but in that bedroom light it looked like real fabric, like velvet, a gown fit for a queen. I had a piece of tape wound around my knuckles, I flexed it as Avra bent to Emil and kissed him, it gave me something to focus on. . . . Sometimes it was so hard to be around them, but where else could I go?

Once or twice I had tried to really think about what I was going to do when they left, driving off to New York or Hilton Head or wherever, driving fast in Avra's car, the taillights blinking, then gone. Wearing their butterfly costumes, twin wings fluttering in the wind, metamorphosing, distance times speed times love. Equals what. And just me, the worker bee, watching them go from the parking lot. . . . And I wouldn't even be in the parking lot, would I? unless I planned to follow them to prom. *Are you going to tag along or what?* I asked myself, staring down at the tape, flexing, clenching. *Are you ever going to do anything on your own?*

• • •

In the fall, I'd be doing everything on my own. Going to Central. Going to classes. Meeting people, like my mom met my dad, like Emil's parents met each other in the lab. Avra would call me from Hilton Head. I'd never see Emil again.

What if I was Avra? Or if Avra was me? Would she try to get between Emil and me? Or would she back off, and just go her own way? Or do something totally different, something I would never think of in a million years? . . . No, that's Shira.

What are you going to do, I asked myself again, but I just couldn't picture it, what would happen when they were gone. It was like a black hole in my mind, like in a movie when the blackboard's full of equations and someone's hand wipes it all clean. And there wasn't anything I could do about it anyway, I couldn't stop them, I didn't want to stop them. So my thoughts would slide away, back to the present, to Emil's frown, the noise of the music, the smell of tape and cigarettes and beer, the minutes slipping away—

"Baby, what happened?" Avra said. She squatted, the dress bunching stiffly around her. "What—oh my god, what did you *do*?"

Emil laughed a little, a weird strained little chuckle, and turned to show us his hand: the palm was cut open, sheared, by the industrial scissors. I saw blood, not a fountain or anything but a lot of blood, way more than we could cope with by ourselves.

"Jesus!" I said. "Emil, what did you *do?*"

"It's nothing, it's—"

Avra stood up so fast she almost fell over. "Get a Band-Aid or something," she said in a funny voice.

"No," I said. "No, this needs stitches. Come on, we have to go to the emergency room. Avra, get your—"

"You guys go," she said. I could barely hear her over Red Cat Orchestra. Her face was an odd color, as if her blood was swimming all around aimlessly under her skin, pink forehead, clammy white cheeks. "You guys—Dana, I just, I can't drive right now, OK? You guys go."

I picked up the first thing I saw—a roll of tape, royal blue tape—and wrapped a strip around Emil's hand, wrapped it hard. I wasn't really thinking, just acting. Then I dug in Avra's purse for her keys—they weren't hard to find, her key ring had about a thousand silver charms and stuffed animals and hole-punched bottle caps dangling from it, the whole thing was as big as your fist—and we hurried downstairs and out to the car. We left Avra upstairs, by the bed, her head leaning on her arm. I had never noticed her get sick about blood before, not even that time she fell off the pier at Tiger Lake and cut her knee almost to the bone.

My heart was beating fast, I was scared, but not terrified, I knew it would be OK. "Does it hurt a lot?" I asked Emil as we backed out of the driveway.

"It isn't really bad," he said, staring at it like it wasn't attached to him, just this taped-up wet thing lying in his lap. He was pale, but he didn't look sick. "It hurts, but mostly it just feels—odd. Like it's . . . buzzing or something." He put the window halfway up with his other hand. "That stupid cardboard. I should have used a razor blade."

And then he started telling me this long story about when he was a kid, how he was trying to make a clubhouse out of a refrigerator box and some old boards, and accidentally stapled his hand to the cardboard. "I just sat there and looked at it for a minute," he said, "just *looked*, like I couldn't believe what I was seeing: My *hand*, with a big silver staple through it." He mimed a totally dropped-jaw stare, like *Huh?* and laughed, and so did I. Our laughter sounded too high, like escaping steam. Pressure. "All I could think was, man, I'm so glad I didn't use the nail gun. . . . Thanks for taping me up, by the way. My hero."

"I didn't do anything really."

"Yes you did. You always do the right thing, Dana."

I almost laughed. *The right thing.* If you knew what I dream about, I thought, you wouldn't say that.

I used to think of that sometimes, what Emil would do if I just said, *I love you. I can't help it. I don't even try to help it. I just—put up with it. Because I love the look on your face right before you laugh, I love to hear you sing to the radio, I love it when you argue with my mom about politics. I love you and I can't stop. Did you know that? No, you didn't. No, you don't. Yes, I do.*

We were almost to the hospital, making the turn off Holland Road, when "Wait," Emil said. "I have to tell you something." He held up his cut hand. In the dash light it looked swollen to me, his fingers especially, and darker than it should have; blood was crusting around the tape. "Forget the hospital for right now, just park for a minute, OK?"

"Emil, no. You need stitches."

He got a funny look on his face then: Pain? Was he scared? "Dana," he said, "I'm not—I don't want to go."

I didn't answer, just kept driving past the hospital, the emergency room entrance, its glowing bright red-and-white sign; past an oil-change place, a florist, a McDonald's, circling back over to Holland as "Stitches aren't that bad," I said, turning toward the hospital again. "I've had them twice, and they don't really hurt that—"

"No," he said. He was looking out the window, away from me. "It's not that. I mean I don't want to *go*. With Avra. It's not—right."

I looked at him, fast, then back at the road as we came to a red light, the transmission making that grinding sound as I put on the brakes too hard. "What did you say?"

He stared down at his hand, wiggled his fingers as much as he could. He didn't answer.

"Emil. What did you just say."

Flat: "I don't want to go," and then fast, fast like when you just want to get something over with, something you know will hurt, "It's *stupid*, Dana, it's such a stupid idea. Just drive away, after prom—it's *stupid*, like something on TV. So we go to New York or someplace, and then what? Sit around and wait for her parents to call the cops? Or for our money to run out, which ought to take like about a week? Jesus! But she doesn't even consider stuff like that, she never does. All she ever talks about is being 'free.' Like she thinks she's in a movie, she's the star of the movie and I'm just like the Boyfriend, and—"

And I'm the Best Friend, the loyal sidekick. I still had the tape on my hand, my knuckles, silver and dull. "Well, have you told her any of this? Have you—"

"No. I mean I try to talk, but she doesn't listen. You know how she is."

But you love her. "Don't you love her?"

He didn't say anything, just kept flexing his hand, wiggling his fingers. Then he leaned over, across the shifter, and kissed me, on the mouth, very fast. I just, I just sat there, I just sat there staring straight ahead. The car behind us beeped, twice, three times, impatient. "The light's green," Emil said. His voice sounded far away.

I pressed on the gas too hard, jerking us forward. McDonald's, florist, oil-change place. Make a left on Holland. He had his head turned toward the window again. Then "I'm sorry," he said. His voice was flat and dry again. "Dana, I'm *sorry*, I didn't mean—"

"It's OK," I said.

I couldn't say how I felt at that moment, I don't think there is such a word. He shifted on the seat, glanced at me, fast, then back out the window; he turned on the radio, turned it off. "We should have been bees," he said, "not butterflies. The costumes, I mean. . . . Smaller wings, less cutting, right?" and he smiled, a small tense smile because he was trying to make a joke, make the moment pass, make a way for us to get safely into the next moment. But I didn't help him, I didn't smile, I couldn't keep pretending. I couldn't do anything but lean over and kiss him back.

His mouth . . . was so soft. His mouth was just so soft.

Avra was out on the front lawn, hunched up and smoking; I could see the bright orange eye of her cigarette in the dark and the green. As I pulled into the driveway, she hopped up and dashed over to the car, hands on the window: "Where's Emil? What *happened*? I called you like a million times—"

"I'm sorry," I said. I could barely look at her. "I had my phone off, I'm sorry. . . . Emil's fine. He's at home, I just dropped him off."

"Well what *happened*? Did he get stitches? What did the doctors say?"

Leaning into the window, her face was right next to mine, her breath smelled like cigarettes. Her eyes were red, she'd been crying. For Emil? Or for herself?

She was my friend, she had been my friend for so long.

"Call him," I said. "He can tell you better than I can."

11

Did he tell her? No. Were we honest? No. But we did the best we could; we tried. But it was already too late. Like metamorphosis. Once you start changing, you've already changed.

The shrine of Aphrodite, the Greek goddess of passion and love, was built in a hexagon shape, like a honeycomb. The High Priestess was called Melissa, which means "bee," and the junior priestesses were called melissae. They practiced a kind of religious sexuality, to celebrate the everlasting fertility of Aphrodite, and the sacred union of earth and sky, with the bee as the representative and the symbol of both.

Overnight there were a million new rules, internal, unspoken rules. We couldn't be in a room alone together. We couldn't sit next to each other at the movies. When we drove around, Avra sang along to the radio; Emil stared out the window; I sat in the backseat with my arms folded. We moved in a cloud you could feel, like a cartoon thundercloud crackling with lightning, swollen up with rain about to fall. Avra felt it too—she had to, how could she not—but she made her own diagnosis. She decided that Emil and I were angry at each other for some unknown reason, so she sat us down at the Green Bowl one day after school to talk it all over: "Come on, you two," she said, sipping her tea. "What the hell's *up*? Whatever it is, let's just talk about it, OK, let's just get it out into the open. And we'll deal with it. There's nothing we can't deal with. Especially now."

Neither of us said anything. Emil stared at the tabletop, tracing his finger in some spilled tea, little figure eights, over and over. I kept flipping a folded strip of duct tape around on my finger, flip-flip-flip. How could it be possible, I thought, to feel this bad and this good at the same time? Shouldn't they cancel each other out, feelings this strong? like a chemical reaction, one element at war with the other? And all the other feelings too, big swirls of guilt and nervousness and, and happiness. And—surprise. You cannot imagine how surprised I was that any of this was happening at all. Flip-flip-flip.

"Come on. It can't be that bad," Avra said, and put our hands together on the table, the way she always did. I pulled mine back so fast I knocked over my water glass.

Emil jumped out of the booth, to the sugar-and-condiment island, yanking napkins out of the dispenser. Lots and lots of napkins.

And then Amy Dane and Kyra Worth came in, and Jason Columello, and they all stopped by our table, and started talking about prom and costumes and wasn't it all going to be so cool. Emil came back, and swabbed at the spilled water with a fistful of napkins. I kept flipping my tape. "Oh," Avra said, "we've almost got our costumes done." She sucked at her straw, a long satisfied slurp. "They're amazing. No one else is going to have anything like it."

Emil slid out of his seat again, going back for more napkins, though we didn't need any more. Jason Columello linked hands with Kyra. He had started growing a beard, a scruffy chin-shrub that looked weird on his round face, like a fake beard in a movie.

"What're you going as?" Kyra asked.

"It's a surprise," Avra said. "You'll see. But it's going to be amazing."

At the napkin island, Emil turned around and looked at me, locked eyes with me: we looked and looked. And Avra didn't see.

When Avra sliced open her knee at Tiger Lake, I held her hands while the EMS guy worked on her; I made the camp director drive me to the hospital, to be with her until her parents could get there. When she broke up with Ty

Jameson at Sadie Hawkins, and he called her a bitch and stormed out of the dance, she said *Be my date, Dana,* and I danced with her all night. When Shira won two Gold Keys in Scholastic for her pencil drawings (and a Silver for a painting, I think), I got three Marx Brothers movies and made Avra watch them all one right after another; she had never seen the Marx Brothers before, she laughed so hard she fell off the sofa and put a crack in the coffee table. When Torie Bishop ripped my LIVE FREE T-shirt on purpose, Avra threw a Coke at her at lunch. When Avra got really drunk for the first time and spent the whole night throwing up, I told her mother I was sure it was the flu, and made her believe me. When Avra plucked Emil out of the quad, I was happy for her, I swear I was. When Avra said I was the sister she had always wished she had, I said she was my sister, too. Even though I had never wanted a sister, not really, I mean I'd never really thought about it. I don't think like she does. I don't—need like she does.

The average lifespan of a butterfly is twenty to forty days. The average lifespan of a queen bee is two to five years, but can be as long as nine. There is no such thing as a queen butterfly.

For five whole days, we were never alone, Emil and I. I hardly talked to him, I barely even looked at him, I was hanging on by my fingertips. Finally, on Tuesday, Avra picked me up to go to the Mayflies concert. I didn't really want to go, even though she said it was just going to be her and me, a night out together like we used to; and I was afraid that she was going to want to "talk," or something. But I didn't have a good excuse to get out of it, and I didn't want to flat-out lie to her, things were bad enough as it was. So OK, let's go see the Mayflies.

"Have a good time," my mother said as I pulled on a jacket; it was chilly out and raining, it had been raining all day, gloomy as winter. "You deserve it."

I just looked at her. I almost laughed. Not at her, but at the whole thing; everything. Like Shira used to say: *Is it funny ha-ha or funny oh-my-god?*

And of course who was there in the passenger seat but Emil, shoulders hunched, his bandaged hand normal-size now, the big hospital wrapping shrunk down to a tidy white band. And "I lied," Avra said. She was smiling in her *I-got-you!* way, like a superior nine-year-old who's just locked you out of the house and is standing there jingling the keys. "We're not going to see the Mayflies. We're not going anywhere. You two are going to stay in this car and talk this thing out, whatever it is, until you make up with each other. Because I am filthy sick of you both, OK? And I don't have time for this bullshit, it's almost prom."

And she turned the engine off and hopped out, dashing through the rain back to my house, to sit and chat with my mother—we could see them in the window—as Emil and I stared at each other, two shadows in the dark. Finally he said, "So why won't you talk to me?"

How is it possible to be so—aware of another person, another human being? to *feel* him, as if he were a living part of me? When I finally answered, my voice sounded funny. Funny oh-my-god. "You know why."

"Well you can't just pretend like you don't—know me anymore. You're so worried about Avra, what about me? How do you think I feel?"

I didn't say anything. I could smell his skin, his own special scent. My hand found his, the unhurt one. He wasn't wearing the spoon ring anymore. We held hands so tightly it was as if our whole bodies were concentrated in our fingers, our palms. Our whole bodies. Rain ran harder down the windows; the glass was fogging up. Then "What about going away?" I asked. "Did you tell her you're not going?"

He looked miserable. "No. I tried to bring it up, but then—you know how she is when she doesn't want to hear something, she started yelling and then she started crying, and, and that was it. Plus I'm a coward. Did you know that? I'm a fucking coward."

I closed my eyes. My thumb stroked the side of his hand, slowly, up and down. "You could still go," I said. "Nothing's changed."

"Yes it has. *Yes*, it has. And we have to—do something, I can't keep on going like this, I want—"

I put my other hand on his mouth, his lips. My eyes were still closed. I could feel his breath on my palm, the heat of it. He kissed my hand. I felt it everywhere. *Don't*, I said, but not out loud.

He moved on the seat, shifting, a rustling sound, then "Dana," he said. "Look at me." I didn't. I couldn't. If I looked at him now I would never leave the car, I would never be able to—

"Dana. Honey. Look at me."

I opened my eyes: *Honey*. He took a picture of me, right then, just as my eyes opened. Like something blooming, someone being born.

"I have to be able to see you," he said. "All the time."

Then he climbed out of the car, into the splattering rain, knocked on the door, and collected Avra. We told her that everything was OK, that we were friends again, that everything was fine. Then we all went to the Green Bowl for take-out tea and drove around and Avra sang songs and Emil looked out the window and I sat in the back with my arms folded.

She dropped him off first, kissing him quick and careless as he climbed out of the car; he didn't look at me. When she pulled up to my house, she gave my forearm a little squeeze and "See?" she said; she was smiling that same nine-year-old's smile. "Aren't you glad I lied to you?"

Would you be glad if I lied to you?

"No," I said.

We had to scramble to finish the costumes, just me and Avra because the cutting was done, the construction of the wings, so it was only tape and fitting now. The wings sat propped in a corner, folded, still, mysterious. They looked like nothing much, just blue-painted cardboard, until they opened, and you saw the lacework of them, the intricate pattern Emil had sketched and cut, before he cut himself. But they were sturdy, too, they moved like real wings, flexed and even flapped. *Aerodynamically correct,* Emil said. They looked as if they could really fly.

Emil mostly sat apart from Avra and me, doodling or staring out the window, or cross-legged on Shira's empty bed. Sometimes our eyes would meet and one of us, mostly me, would look away, drag my attention back to what I was supposed to be doing. Sometimes he would just get up and leave, walk out of the room, the house; we would hear him down on the patio, or we wouldn't hear him at all. Avra would frown and crank up the music. I would keep working, keep ripping tape, or whatever I was supposed to be doing in that moment. Just. Keep. Going.

I never had a problem like this before. I never didn't know what I wanted to do, should do, had to do. There were times when I felt like I was seriously losing my mind, I was completely, what is the word, detached. I'd be talking to Avra, or washing my hair, or answering a question in class, functioning perfectly correctly—while my real mind, my *self*, was somewhere else entirely, having an out-of-body experience. With Emil. Or circling around thinking, like a car stuck in the sand is driving: the wheels are going as fast as they can, but there's no forward motion at all. Every time Avra brought up leaving, how she'd gotten a different map or checked out some new route online or was almost totally decided on New York now, did I know about the Village, it sounded so filthy cool—it was all I could do not to grab her by the arms and say. . . . What. What was there to say? So I didn't say anything, to her or anybody, and got these squeezing kinds of headaches, and woke up too early or couldn't fall asleep. And my mother kept on pestering me, asking me what was wrong: after dinner, in the hallway, first thing in the morning before Avra picked me up—

"Dana, are you all right?" In her baggy old bathrobe, tugging at the sash. "Seriously?"

I'd been up since five o'clock, just staring at the ceiling, at my clock, at the insides of my eyelids. No answers there. "I'm fine."

"Well I'm getting worried about you. I *am* worried—"

"Why should you be worried?"

She frowned. She grew a little wrinkle between her eyes when she frowned, not like Avra's mother did, or even Avra, more like something Emil might have drawn, one little sketch-line that changed her whole face, made her look older, more like a typical mom. "Don't insult my intelligence, Dana. Please."

When she said *please* that way, I had to answer. Is it a total lie when you don't tell all the truth? "OK," I said, hitching up my backpack. "It's just stress, I'm very stressed right now, OK? But it'll be over soon. So don't worry."

The line softened, receded, as she nodded, she thought she knew what I meant: school, or finals, or graduating; I think she thought that. "All right then," she said. "But you'll tell me if there's real trouble, won't you? Promise me." I didn't say anything. "Promise me, Dana."

"I promise."

"All right then." And then she hugged me, around the shoulders, the way Avra sometimes does. But my mother's not a big hugging-type person, not demonstrative, so when she does it, it really means something. Not just *I love you* or *It's OK* or whatever, it means *I am for you. No matter what.*

And just for that second I felt like crying, flash-flood tears hot in my eyes because I wanted to tell her, I wanted to tell *someone*, I wanted someone to tell me what to do—

—but all I did was hug her back, a hard little squeeze,

then *blip-blip* a car horn, car in the driveway because "Avra's here," I said, and left.

In Bio II Mr. Davis stopped me after class and asked if I had anything ready to show him yet: "I have your outline," he said, "but nothing subSTANtial. You know this project is worth a LOT of points, Dana?"

"I know," I said. I hadn't even looked at it since that day, the apiary day. I wasn't even sure where all my notes were. "I'll have it in on time."

"Points deducted for lateness, as always. But I'd hate to see that happen to a project of yours." He gave me a funny look, it took me a second to realize he was trying to be nice. "You know, if there are any special CIRcumstances—family issues, or something like that—the deadline can certainly be FLEXible. But you have to let me know, OK?"

At first I didn't get it, then I did, and "OK," I said, embarrassed, backing away. If even a teacher can see that something's wrong, then everyone can see it. Except Avra. Who asked me to come over that night to finish fitting her prom dress, could I come right after dinner? or for dinner, that would be even better—except not for me because then I had to sit there and pretend to enjoy mushy portobello lasagna while Avra and her mother snapped and snarled at each other and her dad tried to make normal small talk with me—

"So how's your mom doing, Dana? Keeping pretty busy?"

"She's fine."

"I wish *my* mother was fine."

"Don't start, Avra, all right? Just do not start."

—as the tension in the room stoked the tension in my head, my chest, until I felt like I had to get out of there, I just had to get *out*. So I excused myself and sat on the patio, staring at the acacia trees, wondering where Emil was. I hadn't seen him since lunch; he'd mumbled something about errands, something he had to do at home, he would see us later. Us. He looked at me when he said it, then quick back to Avra, who said *Come to my house then, we'll be finishing up my dress.*

My house. *My* dress. *My* boyfriend.

The breeze picked up, fluttering the leaves like wings, swaying the slim branches of Avra's mother's topiary roses, pink and paler pink and white, like little clouds growing on little cloud-trees. Avra's dad came out onto the patio and smiled at me; he looked tired, even more tired than usual. "Too much estrogen in there," he sighed, then looked embarrassed when I laughed. "I didn't mean it that way. It's just when they start in on each other—well, you know how it is, you're practically another family member here."

Another family member, another daughter, Shira and Avra and Dana. . . . What would he think, if he knew about Emil and me? He would hate me, wouldn't he, he'd think *All this time I thought she was Avra's friend, another family member, but now*—And Avra's mother would *really* hate me. And Shira—Shira would survey the whole situation, and then say something calm and pithy that no one else had even thought of. But then probably hate me too. Or at least disapprove of me: for lying. For wanting her sister's boyfriend. Her little sister. . . . Avra's dad was saying something else now, about pruning the acacias, something very dad-like. And I nodded, as if I was listening right along, listening to his problems that were really no problems at all—*maybe blight, have to call the arborist, of course that can get expensive*—in that worried soothing dad-voice, a voice I had never heard at home, or so long ago that it was less a memory than a dream, or like something I read in a book, something nice I liked enough to pretend was really mine.

Would anything be different for me, right now, if I had had a dad? if I had one now, waiting at home? Would he sit on the patio with me and talk over my troubles, give me advice, what would that be like? Would I even want it if I had it? A man around the house. . . . Once a long time ago I asked my mother why she hadn't ever remarried, and she shrugged and said *Well* and *I don't know* and shrugged again and then finally *Your father just—struck sparks,* she said.

What do you mean?

From me, she said. *He struck sparks from me. Even though we couldn't make it work. . . . I guess I never met anyone else who struck sparks like that.*

At the time I hadn't known what she was talking

about, but now I did, I knew exactly what she meant. Emil struck sparks from me, in a way no one else had, no one else had ever come close to. And I struck them from him. Not Avra: me.

"—plans? For this summer, I mean. . . . Dana?"

That dislocation again, that detached two-places-at-once feel, I opened my eyes and closed them, hard enough to make sparkles, opened them again and "I'm sorry," I said. "I was thinking about the acacias. What did you say?"

"I just asked if you and Avra had made any plans yet for the summer. Are you thinking of traveling at all?"

He said it so innocently, hands behind his head, just innocently wondering because well, some friends of theirs had a cabin in Wisconsin, quite a lovely place, if we were interested we could have it for a week or two. "There's swimming, of course, and the boat to take out. Although you girls would probably rather go someplace where there's shopping," he said, and smiled, and I smiled back and thought *Another secret. Another lie.* But it was Avra's lie, Avra's secret so "We haven't made any plans together," I said, which was true. I picked up an acacia stem and twirled it between my fingers, back and forth. "She's mostly worried about prom, you know, getting her and Emil's costume together and, and everything."

He nodded. "Do you—like Emil, Dana?"

My heart immediately started pounding, a fast guilty thump. I made a crooked shrug, he must have seen something weird on my face, I'm sure he did because "I don't mean to ask you to betray a confidence," he said. "I just wonder sometimes if Avra and Emil are too—serious about each other. We never had that kind of problem with Shira, you know, Shira was always dating lots of different boys, never any one kid in particular. Avra did that, too, for a while. But now she seems so—bonded with Emil. And her mother and I worry." He gave me a wistful look. "*She* doesn't think so, I know, but we do worry about her. . . . I trust your opinion, Dana. What do you think of Emil?"

Oh god. What was there to say? what *could* I say? and all of a sudden I wanted to laugh, I *had* to laugh so I tried to make it into a cough, a sharp little bark and "I'm sorry," I said again, and cleared my throat. "Excuse me." My face felt hot, but it was dim out there, he couldn't see; I didn't think he could see. Finally "Emil's a good person," I said. "He would never want to hurt Avra, never."

Then the patio door slid open, we both half turned to look and "Dana," Avra's mom said; the line between her eyes was carved deep. "Her Highness is upstairs, bellowing for you. . . . I'm surprised you can't hear it from out here. I'm surprised you can't hear it in the *street*." She took my seat, and I went inside. As I turned to slide the door closed, I saw Avra's dad put his hand on her shoulder.

Upstairs Red Cat Orchestra was on; Avra was lighting a cigarette when I walked into her room. She usually never smoked when her parents were home but I knew better than to say anything about it, I didn't want to say anything anyway. I didn't want to talk, or hear how she hated her parents, or work on her dress, or even be there, really, but where else was I going to go? and anyway she seemed to be making an effort for once, she was smiling around the cigarette clenched in her teeth and "Let's finish this thing tonight," she said, pulling the dress from its hanger. "It's almost prom. And I'm getting filthy tired of smelling tape, aren't you?"

"A little," I said.

We worked on the skirt, the last overlapping stripes, she played "All the Way to You" over and over, smoking and ripping tape and "I want to see how it hangs from behind," she said. "Tell me if it looks puckered at the neck," and stripped off her T-shirt, her bra, there was a pinkish-purplish mark on one of her breasts, a bruise? or a hickey from Emil? and all of a sudden I was furious, so angry I didn't even know I was angry, it was like I couldn't breathe. How could he kiss her, be with her, stay with her? when he knew he belonged with me? And how could I just stand there and watch it?

"Is it puckered?" she said.

I didn't say anything. I could feel my heart. I could hear my heart.

He struck sparks from me.
Emil's a good person.
Dana. Honey. Look at me.

"Dana?" eyebrows up, looking back at me over her shoulder like a magazine model and "Hey," at the door, hand on the door and it was Emil, wearing his obscurators, half smiling then not smiling then "Hey," again but different, worried, like he could smell it, like ozone, that cartoon storm a real one now, as he looked from me to Avra and back again—

—and I didn't say anything, to him or to her, I just walked right across the room—

—and picked up the wings, the folded blue butterfly wings neatly propped against the closet door like a promise, like something just waiting to happen: and I walked out with them, put them under my arm and walked out, down the hall and down the stairs and out to my mother's car; and leaned them on the passenger seat. As I started the car, Emil crashed out, sunglasses off, calling "Dana! Dana, wait—"

—but I didn't, I drove away, the breeze from the window growing stronger as I got to the highway, stronger still as I hit the expressway and the wings began to move, *aerodynamically correct*, rustling beside me in the wind and the darkness, the sunset a pink and purple smear as I kept driving, as my phone kept ringing, I didn't answer or even look at the numbers, I just kept on: as the warm wind blew my hair back, and fluttered the wings, making a sound like flying, as if they had changed on their own from painted cardboard to living membrane, from the wished-for into the real, from what you want into what you get. Metamorphosis. The cries of the queen, calling for her sisters. . . . I drove like a song you keep singing over and over and over, until my phone stopped ringing, and the traffic thinned, and I was almost completely out of gas. Then I turned around, filled the tank, and flew back.

• • •

When I pulled into my driveway, Emil was sitting on my front porch, waiting for me. It was dark, dark everywhere, but I could see him even before the headlights touched him, before he jumped up. "Dana!"

I slammed the car door. The wings were still in the passenger seat.

"What happened? Where did you *go*? I kept calling you, I—"

"Where's Avra?" I said. My voice sounded very calm.

"At her house, I guess. I don't know. We had a fight." He put his hands on me, on my arms, one arm cooler than the other, from hanging out the window, in the wind. "Why did you run out like that? What happened?"

I didn't answer. I put my hands on him, on his face, my palms to his cheeks, one hand cooler than the other; and I kissed him. I kissed him like honey. I kissed him like the wind. I kissed him like a million wings beating on the air, like a spark struck from pure gold, I kissed him until he couldn't breathe and I let him breathe and then I kissed him again. When I stopped, he was panting a little, like he had run a long way; his whole body was trembling.

"I love you," I said. I didn't even think it first, I just said it, out loud, like something alive in the air: *I love you.*

And then I climbed back in the car, and drove over to Avra's.

It was late, past midnight by now, but her dad was still downstairs; he let me in. He looked as if he wanted to say something, or ask me something, but instead he just smiled, an uncertain kind of smile, like when you think someone has bad news for you but you're willing to pretend that they don't for just a little while longer.

"Is Avra home," I said, not a question because it wasn't a question, I knew she was, her car was in the driveway, a light was on in her bedroom and "She's upstairs," he said. He patted my shoulder as I passed.

Her parents' bedroom door was closed; I could hear the TV. Avra's door was open. The prom dress lay on the floor, heaped up like something that had died where it fell. She was on her sheet-snarled bed, smoking, her face red and blotchy. She had been crying. And drinking, I could smell it.

"What the *hell*," she said, when I pushed in the door, "is going *on*."

I didn't say anything. It was as if I had been breathing some rare gas, smoke from a giant bee smoker, something that made me feel like I was looking through a microscope and a telescope at the same time: at myself, standing there in her room, silent and still; at her. At how messed up she looked, tangled up in the sheets, eyes puffy, tears on her cheeks. The bedside lamp was on, glowing through the blue-green shade, shadow and light on the picture I took of them on Harsens Point, smiling out from the wall like it came with the frame, two strangers I'd never seen before.

"Is everyone crazy now? Is that like the new reality?" Her cigarette smoldered against the sheet; she snatched it away. "First you run out of here, and then *he* runs after you, and then he comes *back* all pissed off—" and she started crying, moans and hiccups, the way a little kid cries. "My dress is ruined, too, it's all ruined, everything's ruined. And the wings, the wings are gone—"

What did she mean? *Everything's ruined, we had a fight,* what did that mean? but I couldn't ask, couldn't stop, could only say what I was there to say which was "Avra," in a very flat voice, as dry and flat as I could make it, because I had made up my mind on the drive, the whole long way there and back, "Avra, listen to me. Listen. I can't be your friend anymore." Because I wasn't going to follow her cries, and track her into her waxy little cell; I was leaving, not running away but pulling back, all the way back, into myself. Because if I stayed, I would have him, I would take him, and that was wrong. Because she was my friend, even if she was selfish and silly and whatever, had been my friend at least; and that was enough. "You just—live your life now, and I'll live mine."

"What?" She looked completely like a kid now, her mouth open, a little girl betrayed who just can't believe it, can't believe such a thing even exists, a *yes* turned into a *no*. A *never*. "What are you talking about? *What* are you *talking*—"

"You have Emil. That's enough." I folded my arms. I kept my voice flat and even. "Don't pick me up for school tomorrow," and I walked out, just like that I walked out and "Dana!" she yelled after me, "DANA!" and then really started crying, howling, I knew her parents could hear no matter how loud the TV was, both the TVs, but did it matter? No. They knew already, or knew something, knew that everything was wrong so I let myself out, I drove carefully home, I carefully parked my mother's car—

—and as I did, I saw the light click off in the kitchen, on in the living room. When I stepped in, she was standing there in jeans and a jacket, her forehead lined; I knew by her face that she was worried, had been worried, had been calling Avra's house, Avra's parents, me on my unanswered phone, had had her jacket on because she was ready to run out somewhere, car or no car, but all she said was "Dana."

And I opened my mouth, I was going to say *What* or *I'm OK* but instead a sound came out, not crying, a sound like something splitting in two and "Dana," she said again, and hugged me, a hug like when I was little, folding me up in her arms. Finally "You promised," she said, letting me go, stepping back far enough to see my face, look into my eyes, "remember? If there was real trouble. Remember?"

So I told her. Not all of it, but some; enough. She hung up her jacket, and we sat at the kitchen table, and she made tea and we drank it, Orange Blossom tea with Treeville Farms honey, and I told her that Avra wanted to go away. That I cared about Emil and he cared about me, so I was the one who was going away, even though I wasn't actually going anywhere. Because we couldn't keep on the way we were, and somebody had to do something about it.

When I was finished talking she let out a sigh, hands around her cup of cold tea. A car went by outside, its music loud in the quiet, *thump-YEAH-thump-YEAH-YEAH*. The clock on the stove said 1:48. Finally she looked me in the face and "You're a good person, Dana," she said. "You always have been. You have a good heart." I remember what Emil said: *You always do everything right.* I didn't say anything. *A good heart*, what did that mean? but I just nodded, like *Yes, I hear you*, and put my cup in the sink, and went upstairs. My body felt heavy as I walked up the stairs, like rocks, like a cave I had buried myself in; my heart. I didn't cry then, either.

Two-eighteen, two-forty, four o'clock; I didn't sleep, just lay on my back thinking. Of Emil, of Avra, of everything, wondering if my phone would ring; it never did. When I saw light, faint then brighter then actual morning, I turned my phone off, and went back downstairs.

The first thing I saw were the wings, set carefully by

the china cabinet, my mother looked up when I came in and "They were in the car," she said. I didn't answer. I never really liked coffee but I had a cup then, hot and black and bitter, I stirred in a teaspoon of honey. My mother filled her travel mug and nodded goodbye, which I was grateful for; I had absolutely nothing to say to anyone, which made it much easier to go to school alone, sit through first hour and second hour, walk head down and weary the hundred miles to third hour where I usually picked up Avra by her locker but instead "Where's Avra?" Kellie Ballister said. She had just gotten her hair colored, a bizarre buttercup-yellow, it looked made out of plastic and terrible. "Did she finally run away from home, or what?"

I shrugged, trying to seem casual. "I don't know." Her seat was empty, but that could mean anything. I knew she hadn't left, she would never go before prom—

—and sure enough I saw her, at lunch in the quad, wearing big pink sunglasses; she made sure that I was looking before she turned her head deliberately away. Kyra Worth was with her, and Jason Columello. And Emil. In his obscurators. Staring straight at the ground.

I had carried the wings upstairs to my bedroom, leaned them carefully against the closet door. They looked so beautiful there; they were beautiful. . . . Why had I taken them? What was that supposed to prove?

In ancient times, the bee was the symbol of immortality, representing the Mother Goddess. A famous image from the Neolithic era shows a female figure with the head of a bee and the feet of a bird. The butterfly was also sometimes used to depict the Goddess. The images of both the butterfly and the bee were often painted or carved onto sacred protective amulets to ward off loss, rejection, loneliness, and grief (Fig. 15). Did they work? History doesn't say. But the power of the object itself might have brought some comfort to the one wearing it, at least for a little while.

Prom was in eight days. Eight more days; eternity. Standing in line at the cappuccino machine Dorie Huber asked me, "Next week is prom or something, isn't it? Are you going?"

"No," I said.

"Won't sully yourself, huh? Me neither. Mike and I are going to the dollar show that night, to see *Vixen Warriors*. Or *Precious the Clown*. . . . Actually a bunch of us are probably going, come with us if you want."

"Thanks," I said. Dorie stepped up to get her cappuccino. From the corner of my eye I could see them, across the cafeteria, I couldn't help it. Like I saw them in the halls, sitting together in the quad, Avra's car whooshing by after school, the transmission grinding away. I tried not to look, but you can't go blind just because you want to.

Although Avra had; blind inside. To understand what I did—and I didn't blame her, I didn't exactly let her down gently, or tell her the truth, I didn't do any of it the right way, just the only way I could—she made up a story, and tried to force me into it, make the puzzle pieces fit whether they actually did or not.

First she called; I never answered. Then she e-mailed; I deleted. She stuck notes in my locker; I didn't read them, I threw them away still folded up. Finally she roared up after school, walked in and plopped down at the kitchen table, smoking—even though my mother doesn't allow anyone to smoke in our house and Avra knows it—and informed me that she knew *exactly* what my problem was, what my problem obviously always *had* been, and what a coward and a bitch I was not to just come out and tell her that "You really think you're better than me," she said, blowing smoke. She was wearing a Too Many Roses T-shirt with hacked-off sleeves, she had cut them crooked so they hung tattered against her arms, like she'd been in some kind of fight and barely escaped. "You look down on me. Probably you always did. That's why when I talked about leaving, you never said anything to help me, not one single thing. . . . Like Shira. You're a lot like Shira, you know."

Her worst possible insult, but I didn't say anything. Which only made her madder, made her louder, made her mash her cigarette out in the empty blue checkerboard nut-dish and immediately light up another one. "All that time, hanging out with me, pretending to be my friend—"

"I wasn't pretending."

"What?"

"Nothing."

" 'Nothing.' Right. And now, when I need you the most, when everything's all, all screwed up and crazy, when I need someone I can depend on, you just walk away. *That's* a real friend. That's a real *sister.*"

"I'm not your sister," I said.

"Well you act just like her." Her eyes were glassy, shiny with tears, she snatched up her jangling fistful of keys, her purse and "Emil hates you now, too," she said, pushing away from the table. "He won't even say your name."

"Do you hate me?"

I don't know what she saw in my face then, I don't even know why I said it. Maybe because I didn't want her to hate me, I didn't want this to have happened, I didn't know how to be her friend and be all my self too. Maybe I never had. But she stopped, there in the doorway, she looked at me and I looked at her and "You were my best friend," she said. She was crying, but she didn't seem to know it, the tears just fell, blue mascara dribbling down her cheeks. "My *best friend.*"

"I know," I said, because I did know. "I'm sorry." I wasn't crying, but I felt tears in my eyes, tiny and hot, like the very first drops of a very big storm. "Avra, believe me, I'm sorry—"

"I don't believe you. Not anymore." She was almost out the door before she stopped, turned on her heel and "The wings," she said, in a different voice. "Our wings, you took them, give them back. We need them."

We. Two halves of a whole. Was that true? No. Oh please no. But then why hadn't he called me, tried to get in touch with me, why hadn't he done anything at all? And if he wasn't ever going to, would I still have done what I did?

Yes.

So I got the wings, and I gave them back. They were never mine, anyway.

That night Avra's mom called, to talk to me, but my mother took the call instead. It seemed to last a long time, my mother silent mostly, but when she spoke her voice was firm; I couldn't hear all the words, but enough—*unfortunate* and *between Dana and Avra* and *Ruth, I said no*—to know that she was mad. Afterwards she came up to my room, just as firmly up the stairs, hand on my door—"Dana?"—and I braced myself, now what? but "Do you know where the downstairs remote is?" she said, and that was it.

Sometimes I am just so thankful that I have my mother for a mom.

You can only live through things day by day, sometimes minute by minute, so *Just get through this week,* I told myself. By the end of it prom would be over, and things would change, maybe not for the better but at least things would be different: Avra would go, or they both would, and it would be over. No, never over. But done. Avra, my best friend—*that* Avra was long gone already. Who was left? The hateful Avra, sitting in the cafeteria, in the quad with her pink sunglasses, with Amy Dane and Kyra Worth, and Jason Columello hanging on her every word. And Emil, who never looked up from his notebook. . . . *It's stupid, it's a stupid idea;* he said that; he meant it, too. But people do stupid things sometimes.

Morning again, waking up, bracing myself for another awful day but then I realized it was Saturday, no school to suffer through, I wouldn't have to see any of them—especially at SavMor, buying conditioner, standing there staring at the shelves and thinking *Could it possibly make any difference whatsoever if my hair is SuperSilky or Soft-'n'Free?* when around the corner came Avra's dad, frowning, pausing by the dandruff shampoo. For a second I thought Avra would appear, too, but when she didn't, when he just kept squinting at bottles I said, "Hi," before I could stop myself, because, I don't know. Because I wanted to see if there was anything left, anything at all. Because people do stupid things sometimes.

He turned, surprised, and said "Dana?" and then "*Dana,* hello," like normal, friendly like normal; almost. We stood in the middle of the aisle, both gripping our bottles, shampoo and conditioner and "How are you," he said, "how's it going? Getting ready for the big day?"

I nodded, not knowing if he meant prom or commencement or what, and he kept talking, a little faster than normal, something about taking a trip, Shira and her urban archaeology of course and then "Greece," he said, "with both the girls, you know—maybe Avra told you—"

And then he stopped, and I stopped nodding and pretending to smile, and his face changed as "I don't know what happened with—with everything," he said; his voice changed, too, got softer, slower. "But you two are definitely on the outs now, you and Avra?"

The outs. I'd never heard that before, that phrase but "Yeah," I said. *The outs*: the outskirts, the outlands, where you go when you're not in anymore. "We are."

He sighed. "Well. I thought—" and then stopped; he wasn't going to tell me what he thought. "Well, I hope—" but he couldn't tell me that either because right then Avra's mom turned the corner of the aisle, stopping dead halfway down to stare at him, at me and "I'd better go," he said. "See you," and walked away, walked over to her, showed her the dandruff shampoo, but she wasn't looking at him, she was still staring at me and I thought, *She knows.* I don't know why I thought that, but I knew I was right, I felt a rush of heat to my face but I kept staring back at her, at the meanest stare I'd ever seen her use, meaner than Avra at her very worst, until finally she turned her head, slowly and deliberately, like closing a door forever, slamming it, locking it—

—and I turned, too, walked the other way, past the hair spray and the gel, the pyramids of soda and tortilla chips, kept walking until I was almost out of the store and I realized that I hadn't even paid for the conditioner. Oh great, I thought, get arrested for shoplifting, too, why don't you? That would make this week complete.

• • •

I knew that people at school were talking about me, the Amy Dane–Kyra Worth people, saying every dumb thing you could think of, but I didn't care about that. What I cared about was Emil, ghosting after Avra, sitting like a zombie in the quad, Emil who never called me, not even once. Did he think that I didn't want him anymore? *I love you.* No, he couldn't think that. My mother said he came over, twice, nervous, she said he looked nervous. And tired. *Like he isn't sleeping,* she said. *Raccoon rings under his eyes.* But both times I was gone. Did he know before he came that I wouldn't be there? Did he have something to tell me he didn't want to say?

In Greek mythology, bees were considered messengers of the divine, so their sacred nectar, honey, was brewed into mead, a mildly alcoholic drink, for the seers at Delphi to drink, to allow them to prophesy. The high priestess, the actual Oracle of Delphi, assumed the name "Queen Bee," some believe to emphasize her power to foretell the future. The Viking goddess Gonlod, called the Mother of Poetry, also brewed mead in her cauldron, to inspire all seekers of true visions. Many cultures believed that truth can be found in the hive.

Five days, three days, two days. How can time move so slowly? How can days be so long? I didn't talk to anyone at school, or anywhere, I didn't do any homework, I just worked on my bee project; it was really all I did. Research more ancient cultures, redo two of the charts, carefully crop and resize all the pictures Emil took: the antique skeps, the open, living hive. I didn't print all the pictures, some I kept just for myself, even though I couldn't look at them anymore; but I couldn't throw them away either, even though they hurt me. Like a stinger, wedged deep under my skin.

And I made wings. Bee wings, like the butterfly's, meticulously sketched in pencil then in Sharpie then cut out of refrigerator-box cardboard—but I didn't slice myself, I used an X-Acto knife, I was very careful. When they were cut out I painted them with acrylic paints, and then assembled them. They were perfect, and perfectly to scale, they even worked like a real bee's wings: if there was a four-foot bee he, she, could have used my wings to fly to South America. And back again.

So I was done.

The night before prom I couldn't sleep, I didn't even try to, I just lay in my bed like a bee in her cell. As soon as it was morning, as soon as the sun was up, I stepped quietly downstairs, found the keys, and took my mother's car to school. It was so early that no one else was there yet but the swim team yawning and shuffling toward the pool, and the rugby people yelling faintly in the back fields. I walked through the clean and empty halls, shiny buffed floors, bare trash cans, all the signs for prom, COME TO BAL MASQUE!! carrying my wings wrapped up in newspaper, and a folder tucked under each arm, one for the graphs, one for the actual project. For a second I thought, *What if Mr. Davis isn't in yet?* What would I do with my stuff? The wings wouldn't fit in my locker. But he was there in his room, checking e-mail and drinking a take-out coffee; he looked surprised to see me, to see anybody that early, probably.

"I brought my project," I said. He took the folders, then watched as I carefully unwrapped the wings, his eyebrows raised but "You said be creAtive," I said; I tried not to say it in his voice, but I must have failed because he looked at me sharply, but then smiled, a little.

"Well you're certainly THAT, Dana. And you're two days late, so that's, um—"

"Twenty points off," I said.

"Twenty-five. Tomorrow it would have been fifty," scratching on one folder with his pen. I showed him how the project was organized, the pictures, the graphs; I showed him how to work the wings, to make them larger, then smaller. "They're aerodynamically correct," I said.

"ImPRESSive," he said. He made them flap a couple of times. "You put in some real WORK here, didn't you?"

"I did," I said. It was harder than it looked, even. All of it. "I really did."

Then I left. I left him with the wings and the folders and I walked right out of school, something I had never actually done before, not like that, just walking in and walking out, as if I was done with that, too. When I got home I dropped my mother's keys back in her purse—she was in the shower—crawled into my bed and went immediately to sleep, as if the whole thing had been a dream. I was just waking up again when my phone rang, my mother calling, her voice tense: "Dana? Dana, are you all right? What's happening there?"

I sat up in bed. The light past my window was strong

and very bright, slanting the other way now: afternoon light. "Nothing," I said. My voice was a little rough from sleeping, I had to clear my throat and say it again. "Nothing. Why?"

"School called. They said you were absent without permission, but one of your teachers said he'd seen you come in earlier. What's going on?"

"Nothing. I had to go turn in my Bio project." I didn't say anything else, and she didn't say anything, for about a minute. That's a long time to be quiet on the phone. Finally "All right," she said, a little too casually. "Are you going back, then?"

"Not today. Can I use your car later?"

Another silence, not quite as long. "All right. I'll be home by four . . . Dana, are you—OK?"

"No. But I'll survive."

She sighed, not for me to hear but I heard it anyway, a tight little exhalation; what was she thinking? That I was going to quit school and run off and kill myself or something? Parents worry way too much. Even my mother. "All right," she said for the third time. "I'll see you at four, then."

It was a beautiful day, sunshiny and warm and perfect. Prom day. By now they were all home from school and calling each other, rushing off to the salon, buying condoms and bottles of champagne. Who was going to help Avra attach that wing to her dress? Who was going to help

Emil with the corsage? Who was going to explain to Avra's parents what had happened, when morning came, and no one came home? . . . All those things that used to be mine.

This time I found the exit for the road to Treeville Farms with no problem. At first, I thought no one was there, even though there was a pickup truck parked in the driveway, but finally Mitch came out, a paper napkin in his hand: "I was just sitting down to dinner, actually," he said. He smelled like pizza; he looked surprised to see me again, surprised and puzzled. "Did you have some more questions, or—?"

"I just want to see the bees," I said. It came out sounding slightly insane, although I didn't feel insane. I didn't feel anything, except that I wanted to see those bees one more time.

"Oh. OK, well, if you want to open the hives, I have to go with you. But if you can wait a little bit, until I finish my dinner—"

"No, that's all right," I said. "I don't want to disturb them. Or you. I just want to watch them flying around."

And I did. I sat on the grass, in the midst of the flowers, the clover and lavender and dandelions going to seed, purple and blue and white, watching the bees rise and settle, persistent from flower to flower, getting what they needed. They didn't really notice me, although they flew close by a few times, checking me out. I wasn't a virgin, but I didn't get stung.

• • •

The sun moved down the sky. Dinnertime, shadows, twilight. They would be dancing now, the King and Queen of Hearts, Marie Antoinette and her king; both halves of the butterfly. I wished I could have seen how that costume turned out.

Almost full dark now. Mosquitoes kept landing on me, biting my arms; I kept flicking them away. Eventually Mitch came out again: "Uh, we close, you know, at night, the farm does." He was smiling, but you could tell he couldn't figure out what I was there for, and really wanted me to leave. So I thanked him and got up. The smell of the grass, the heat still in the air, the flowers: it was so peaceful and so sweet. "My project came out great," I said as he walked me back to my car. "I know I'll get an A."

"Well good for you. With all this interest, maybe you ought to look into apiculture as a career." He gave me another little jar of honey, and waved as I drove away, brisk down the gravel road, throwing back soft ghostly plumes of dust.

But I didn't go far. After about a half mile I stopped, and very very slowly, in the settling swirl of dust, backed up until I could just see the Treeville Farms buildings. Then I got out of the car, and walked quietly back to the hives. I had a little penlight in my pocket, but I never clicked it on.

In Minoan culture, the bee represented the soul and its eventual rebirth. In ancient Greece, they embalmed the dead in large urns filled with honey, their bodies curled up in the fetal position, waiting to be born into their next life. Perhaps they were thinking of the life of the hive itself, which just keeps going on eternally, bee by bee by bee.

It got colder than I expected, sitting out there in the grass. All the bees had gone into the hive, of course; they don't fly around at night. Mitch came out of his house once or twice, to do one last chore or another, but he never saw me. I had on a dark T-shirt, I crouched so I almost hugged the ground. It was easy, really; I know how to hide.

Quiet, then even more quiet, only the crickets, and the faintest motion of the leaves. Finally, all alone in that pure quiet, I cried. I cried so hard my throat hurt. I cried so hard I felt like I was turning inside out. Who was I crying for— Emil? Avra? All three of us? Myself? My tears stung me.

I didn't know I had fallen asleep until I woke up, confused in the dark, *where am I?* until I felt the prickle of the grass beneath me, and remembered. My legs were stiff and so dead I had to pinch them to make them feel before they could move. The lights in the outbuildings were all turned off now, only one security light above the back door still burning pale green. When I could stand, I walked quietly down the driveway, then more quickly back to the car. It was like walking in a fairy tale, the arch and sway of the trees in the breeze, no light except the glow of the moon. Little things heard me coming long before I saw them, and hurried away into the weeds. I had half a bottle of water in the car, and a little sample-size bottle of white wine, like you get on a plane, that I had taken from the kitchen. I was going to use it to toast the bees, but I'd forgotten to carry it to the hive. I toasted them anyway, there on the dark road: "To the bees," I said. My voice sounded too loud in the stillness. I whispered, "To the queen," and drank down the whole little bottle. The wine tasted kind of odd, an astringent taste, like very expensive mouthwash; maybe it was going bad. The water was lukewarm; I drank that, too. Then I got in the car and drove home.

It was almost three o'clock by the time I pulled into the driveway; all the lights in the house were off. I had told my mom where I was going, before; she hadn't asked any questions except *When will you be back?* I told her I wasn't sure, but probably late.

Parked in front of the house was a car I didn't recognize at first, a small black sports car, a Mercedes and "Hey," Emil said. He unfolded himself from the driver's seat, holding a paper in his hand, wearing a white T-shirt and his multicolored taped-up tux pants. "Hi."

"Hi," I said. "Where's your costume?"

"That stupid jacket's like an oven," he said. "Like body armor, ha-ha; remember? . . . Can I please sit down?"

I sat on the steps and he sat on the other side, then scooted over to the center and took my hand and examined it like he'd never seen a human hand before or my hand anyway.

"The prom sucked," he said.

"Where's Avra?"

"At the hotel." He shook his head. "Her stupid transmission finally broke, and her dad had to call us a tow truck. We stood there on Highland Road for like half an hour, dressed like a butterfly. People were beeping at us, yelling stuff, it was ridiculous. We started screaming at each other. . . . So I ended up driving," nodding towards his mom's car. "Where did you go?"

"I went back to see the bees," I said.

It was so weird and so casual, like we had just seen each other an hour ago. It was so—normal.

"I was going to tell her," he said. He looked up at the sky, the quiet dark, then down again at our hands. "That one day, when you guys were finishing up the costume, I was going to say *I can't go away with you*. Or—be with you. At all. But then you walked out, and she was—she got all—" He bit his lip. "I still wanted to take her to prom, I mean I didn't want to, but—I promised I would. I promised her. So I had to."

With his free hand he fluttered the piece of paper. "I made this for you, before. When we went to the bee-place, what do you call it? the apiary? But I couldn't give it to you then."

I took it. I couldn't see that well in the dark but I could see enough.

"That day when you, when you said *I love you*, I thought, *This is the best day of my life, and the worst day. Because now I know for sure.* But then you ran away. All this time, Avra and all her big plans, and then you're the one who runs away."

"I had to," I said.

"Can I kiss you?" And he did, not like I had done that day in the driveway, but softly, and for a long time. I could taste candy, and alcohol, and the secret taste of his mouth. Inside me it felt like a dam was bursting, a slow-motion, beautiful dam. Finally we stopped, and he put his arm around me and I put my head on his shoulder, as if it was the natural thing to do, as if I had done it that way every day of my life.

"Why did you kiss me in the car?" I said. It was a whisper.

"I had to," he said. "I love you," he said. "You knew that, right?"

I didn't say anything. The drawing in my hand was damp. I raised my head and kissed him again.

At school it was so strange: same place, different world. Emil and I didn't go around hanging on each other, we didn't have any of the same classes anyway, and besides, we didn't need to, we could pass in the hall, touch hands, and be all right. People talked about us—I heard a little of it, I couldn't help but hear—but nobody ever cares about your life as much as you think they do.

And there was so much else to talk about, like who got crazy-drunk at prom, who got pulled over, who did what to who where. . . . Avra had gone to the hotel with Kyra Worth and Jason Columello, after she ditched Emil during the dance, no ride home and no car and anyway she hadn't packed any suitcases or gathered up any maps, she wasn't really ready to go anywhere. Except to Greece, with her family. And with Jason Columello, apparently, Jason who followed her around now as if he'd never had a girlfriend before, his new Queen of Hearts, her new Emil. . . . You can learn a lot sometimes, through gossip. Which was good, since it wasn't like I could ask Avra anything myself.

Avra wasn't mean to Emil, or rude; she made a point of saying hi to him, especially when she was draped all over with Jason. With me it was different: she didn't say hi, she didn't avoid me, she just acted as if I completely did not exist, the way a little kid would: *If I don't see you, you're not really there.*

It didn't make me mad, or even sad. I just missed her. It sounds funny to say, probably, funny oh-my-god, or like a lie. But I did. Not Avra the way she was now, but the way it used to be. But that was over, had been over for a long time, hadn't it? Not because of Emil. Because of me. If I had been somehow—different, we might still be friends.

Why did you say you wanted to go away? That was the one thing I wanted to ask her. But the more I thought about it, the more I already knew the answer.

Afternoon commencement practice, the stuffy auditorium, the AC kept clicking on then cycling off and it was even hotter backstage in the hallway to the ladies' room, hot and humid and still. I brushed my damp hair, sweat on my forehead, pushed at the door and almost hit a tall shadow pushing in—

—Avra—

—and just like that, that simple and dumb, there we

were, all alone, face to face in the heat and the stillness and "Hi," I said. I expected her to ignore me, go right past me, but she didn't. She didn't do anything but stare.

"How are you?" I said.

She pursed her lips and kept on staring, as if she was a thousand miles away, as if I was something she couldn't quite bring herself to focus on until "Great," she said. "I'm great." She looked great; she looked amazing. She'd gotten her hair cut again, very very short and layered around her face; she had a fresh smooth caramel tan. "I'm going to Greece for two weeks. With Jason."

"And to Acosta," I said, trying to make it sound like a question, but it didn't, it wasn't.

"You always know everything, don't you, Dana?" She leaned so close I could smell her cigarette breath, I could see the shine of her eyes. "Do you know what I think of you, right now?"

I did. I knew exactly what she thought of me, what she always would: as Shira, another Shira, another sister destined somehow for something big; a big sister, not like her. Never her. And she was right. In my head I'd always said she was a queen. In my heart I saw she wasn't, never had been, never would be.

Do you think I didn't know that? Do you think I didn't know what I had done?

"You know, you can have Emil," she said. "I was through with him anyway, I'm not really into drawing little pictures. Or going on stupid Sunday drives to look at bugs."

"Avra—"

"That stupid costume looked like *shit*, by the way. It was hot as an oven and the fucking wings kept falling off. Emil looked like a total clown."

"Avra, listen—"

"No, Dana, *you* listen." She put her hand on the ladies' room door. She wore a big new ring, chunky gold with shiny silvery chips; from Jason? "You're the one who didn't want to be friends anymore, remember? So don't say anything, don't talk to me, all right? Just. *Go. Away.*"

To be a queen you have to act like a queen. I let her go.

Commencement was actually a lot more fun than I expected it to be. They held it at the McArthur Pavilion, this huge outdoor concert hall with formal gardens, and fountains, and a band shell and seats built right into the hill; it's extremely picturesque. Amy Dane wore such incredibly high spike heels that she could barely teeter down the aisle, and she kept getting stuck in the grass. Emil called her Divot Girl. The school orchestra played, all the juniors laughing and joking with each other, seniors now. Kellie Ballister sang a solo about the Gates of Time swinging open, or shut, I couldn't hear all the words. Dorie Huber was salutatorian, after all, and gave a funny, deadpan speech about student activism, "Why You Should Care About Someone Other Than Yourself at Least Once a Year (Besides Christmas)." My mother clapped like crazy when I crossed the stage; Emil shouted out my name, and when it was his turn, I shouted for him. When Avra crossed the stage a ton of people clapped and cheered, and Jason and his friends hooted air horns, even though air horns were supposedly banned; Kyra Worth and her friends yelled and groaned. Avra's mom shouted the loudest, just like she had for Shira when she graduated.

Shira wasn't there, but she'd sent a huge bouquet of roses for Avra—and, surprise, a tiny one for me. Avra's dad carried it over afterwards, as we all milled around on the dark green slope of the lawn, twilight again, car horns honking, everyone hugging everyone else and "It's from Shira," he said, handing the bouquet to me.

Delicate off-white tea roses and a cloud of baby's breath, all wrapped in elegant silver-and-teal paper: the school colors, very clever and thoughtful, just like Shira and "It's gorgeous," I said. It smelled wonderful, too, sweet and a little bit spicy, as if it would be delicious to eat. There was no card with it. "Tell her thank you from me, OK?"

"Will do." He was smiling, but not a total smile. Emil stood a couple of steps behind us, talking to my mom. Avra's dad glanced at him and then away, back at me as "Well," he said, "congratulations, Dana. It's a very big day for you kids."

"It is, yeah, thank you." We looked at each other. I could tell he didn't know what to say, and I didn't either. I had always liked him; he had liked me, too. *Another family member.* "Have a good trip to Greece," I said.

"Will do." He patted my shoulder, an awkward little pat, and walked away, back to the big moving shouting circle of Avra's mom and their relatives, and Jason and his friends, and Avra right in the center, flushed and beautiful and talking too loud—"Acosta, it's such a huge party school, I can't wait"—and waving her giant bouquet.

She wouldn't have liked it in New York, anyway. Or Savannah. And at Acosta, she'd have Shira again.

The picture Emil drew, the one he gave me that night on my porch, is tacked up on my bedroom wall, right over the light switch; I see it every time I walk into and out of my room. It's from when we went to Treeville Farms, the photo Mitch took of us standing underneath the honeysuckle. We're both smiling, just the way we were in the original, but in Emil's drawing, we've got antennae, and we're holding hands. Underneath it he copied some lyrics from a Red Cat Orchestra song:

The girl gives
What the girl requires
Watch her now flyin' higher and higher

And signed it *Love you, Emil.*

Now "You ready?" Emil said in my ear, his breath tickling-warm on my skin. Emil's parents were taking us out to dinner, my mom, too, at a very expensive Japanese restaurant they loved. Then we were going to a party at Dorie Huber's, an all-night party but we weren't going to stay all night, we were going to go off on our own. All our own. . . . His mortarboard was on crooked; I fixed it. Little tufts of hair stuck out on each side. Dorie Huber rushed by—"See you guys at the party"—as "One more picture of you two," my mother said, taking the bouquet from me, and raising her camera. We stood together, Emil and I, then raised our opposite arms high, diplomas in hand. The sleeves of our gowns billowed lightly in the breeze, they shimmered and floated like wings.

The bee is part of folklore all around the world, fairy tales and myths and nursery rhymes and old wives' tales. One says that all bees are born from the body of a bull. Another says that the noise of iron and steel clashing together will make agitated bees settle back into their hive; this is called "tanging the swarm." Another says that a bee's sting directly on the lips is what first brought poetry into the world of humans. The pain she inflicts, says this myth, is equal to the worth of the wisdom she inspires. This is called "kissing the bee."